SCHADENFREUDE

CHRIS KELSO

Dog Horn Publishing

Published by Dog Horn Publishing, England
Dog Horn Publishing
45 Monk Ings, Bristall, Batley WF17 9HU
United Kingdom
doghornpublishing.com

ISBN 978-1-907133-39-8

UK Destribution by Central Books
99 Wallis Road, London, E9 5LN
United Kingdom
orders@centralbooks.com
Phone: +44 (0) 845 458 9911
Fax: +44 (0) 845 458 9912

Non-UK Distribution by Lulu Press, Inc
3101 Hillsborough Street, Raleigh, NC 27607
United States of America
purchaseorder@lulu.com
Phone: +1 919 459 5858
Fax: +1 919 459 5867

Designed by John Eckert

For Karen and Gordon

PRAISE FOR SCHADENFREUDE...

- Chris Kelso is a writer of wide and varied obsessions. In Schadenfreude he shares all of them. Like all possessed minds, his is glued together with recurring themes, and they unify this volume in strange ways. Most forms of transportation in Kelso's world comprise metal peanut shells. And anything tubular, say a transportation artery or a sewer is presented as "ropy," like the blood vessels into which drugs are constantly being injected. He populates Hell with pop icons (for which favour much gratitude is due). And he has performed the heretofore seemingly impossible task of coming up with interesting and original names for punk bands and their songs. This collection is just the right amount of raunchy, and is guaranteed to uplift the heart of today's most discerningly jaded nihilist"

- Tom Bradley, author of *Hemorrhaging Slave of an Obese Eunuch*

"Schadenfreude is more than a short story collection; it's a way of life"

- Stewart Home, author of *Red London*

"Chris Kelso is the one your mother warned you about. He is a sick, sick man - bereft of cure and heaped with symptom. His words will taint you irrevocably. Your eyes will want to gargle after reading just one of his stories. His book is unique - and that's a good thing."

- Steve Vernon, author of *Nothing To Lose*

'Chris Kelso is a writer of almost intimidating intelligence, wit, and imagination. On every page there is evidence of a great mind at work. Just when you're wondering if there are actually still writers out there who still feel and live their ideas out on the page, I come across a writer like Kelso, and suddenly the future feels a lot more optimistic. I look forward to seeing what he's capable of in the longer, novel form: it's a tantalising prospect. To wear his influences as smartly as he does - one calls to mind Burroughs, and Trocchi's more verbose offerings - whilst remaining uniquely himself, in a writer as young as he is, is a very encouraging sign: one of maturity that belies his youth. I look forward to reading more from him in the near future.'

- Andrew Raymond Drennan, author of *The Immaculate Heart*

"Schadenfreude proves, once and for all, that Chris Kelso is NOT a mannequin."

- D. Harlan Wilson, author of *Peckinpah*

"Sparky, modern, avant-garde but accessible, Chris Kelso's book is reminiscent of the most successful literary experimentation of the 60s and 70s, the sort of work that was published in the later New Worlds, but it's also thoroughly contemporary, intimately engaged with modern life as it is right now. Kelso steams with talent and dark wit and his blend of anarchy with precision is refreshing, inspiring and utterly entertaining..."

- **Rhys Hughes, author of *Mister Gum***

- 'This emerging journeyman of the macabre has wormed his way into my grey-matter and continues to seep noxious ichor. I feel like I must devour him. Every little bit of him.'

- **Adam Lowe, author of *Troglodyte Rose***

"Chris Kelso is the finger inside of your least favourite hole giving you your most favourite sensation; Schadenfreude is the frothy evidence left behind."

- **Christy Leigh Stewart, author of *Terminally Beautiful***

"Choke down a handful of magic mushrooms and hop inside a rocket ship trip to futuristic settings filled with pop culture, strange creatures and all manner of sexual deviance. The mundane becomes the bizarre, the standard evolves into the alien, and penises and vaginas are rarely what they seem. Buckle up. Shadenfruede is indeed pleasure derived from the misfortunes of others."

- **Richard Thomas, author of *Transubstantiate***

"Take Mr Kelso's front-loaded disclaimer of dour grey moroseness with the boulder of salt it deserves. This is a jittering nightmare collection of images and events that will startle and delight you at every turn. Revolting and eerily charming, Schadenfreude will linger in your mind long after you put it down."

- **Deb Hoag, author of *Crashin' the Real***

"A bewildering manuscript written in an unknown tongue and cheek. Full of pleats and petards but does not mention halibuts in any context. So don't just read it upside down; read it upside down and inside out."

- **Justynn Tyme; *The don doo-dad of dada***

"The stories in Schadenfreude are like non-Euclidean geometry: mysterious, unique and wrapped in an aura of magic and mysticism. Kelso's prose is lean and tough and the impact these stories have on the reader prove there's no need for gimmicks when the power of weirdness is effectively wielded."

- **Gabino Iglesias – Horror-Talk**

"I hella dug it! Chris Kelso's Schadenfreude is dirty, dark, and fun. This collection is a dismal delight, peppered with humor as black as plague and infused with gripping horror, for fans of macabre fiction."

- Jonathan Moon, author of *Heinous*

"Schadenfreude functions as a pathology museum never intended for those seeking to educate themselves about what may go wrong in fiction--or the world at large--but was instead constructed for the voyeur who escaped from your basement, still bound with razorwire, desperate for the ultimate degradation."

- John Edward Lawson, author of *SuiPsalms*

INTRO

Thanks to the publisher…

- You all like reality television right? As a loyal slave to my own moroseness, when Dog Horn Publishing agreed to provide me with the perfect platform for which to communicate this dour groundswell of opinion, my debut short story collection was only ever going to turn out one way – morose and dour, self-indulgently so. If this collection were a colour, it'd be the gunmetal grey of a sunken barge. If it were a person, it'd be much maligned.

It is the morbid curiosity of ancient Rome.

I am not a misogynist, although these stories are often set a world which is brutally, repulsively masculine.

The mere cosmic fluke which saw "Schadenfreude" published is incidental, I finally have that platform! Now watch me abuse my position atop this glorious literary pedestal like a megalomaniacal drill sergeant punishing his platoon with unrelenting sadism – "terminate with extreme prejudice". A nightmare dawning on a Disney classic. An inbred baby stuck in the heart of amphetamine psychosis. Like a Nazi salute to the Untermunchen, this publisher completely condones me. Know this and look on, gawk eyed and powerless as I transmit the most hideous personalities and scenarios to you in shards of telekinetic cruelty, all thanks to Dog Horn…

I doff my hat to you.

CONTENTS

MEN OF THE HEARTH

Terra 5: An offshore platform blasted in rust by a rippling sea of oil. From land the copper plate initials D-MON CORP are visible hovering over the artificial island construct.

A boat approaches the rig leaving a blaze of foam in the wake of its rear propeller. On board is Floyd Wakewater, future heir of D-MON CORP. His father is ill, trapped in a heavy coma between life and death. Wakewater Jr is in charge of company affairs until his father's recovery.

At the main rig a team of grizzled crewmen, scaffolders and welders are stood waiting to greet Mr Wakewater. Rain beats down relentlessly, the air embittered by the inevitable probability of frost. The boats coxswain tosses up a rope ladder, which a crewman then ties to a railing. They make their way onto the platform. Mr Wakewater dusts off his immaculate suite and addresses the seamen.

- My father is concerned.

One of the men, a small bearded toolpusher, gulps.

- He believes someone is mining unessential resources from the planets core. That was never my father's intention.

Another bearded worker, a man of certain rank, decides to speak up.

- If I may Mr Wakewater, we have a good team here. I've worked with most of these men for decades. We do what we're told and nothing else.

- Is that so?

Wakewater clicks his fingers and the coxswain materialises a suitcase. He forwards it to his superior. Wakewater clicks the case open and brings out a stack of data papers. He grins at the workers like an old sea-dog who's seen all their tricks before.

- This is a document retrieved from last year's expenditure account. According to this, you guys have spent over 40 billion on excess equipment. That's high power drills, wire-lines, pump hangers…the list goes on. You've been sinking boreholes in over 50 different basin sites. Just what exactly are you guys trying to find down there?

There is a pregnant pause then a reluctant sigh.

- It's not what we're trying to find sir; it's what we've already found…

- I don't understand.

- Come with me sir…

The workman leads Wakewater down into the massive centrifuge basement. The corridors are lit with red blubs and shadows cascade across the iron cast like frantic spirits. The bearded worker of rank begins explaining himself. Outside the rain is still lashing down.

- We were taking core samples in the new region, like we were told to, when we came across an…anomaly.

- An anomaly?

A sprawling behemoth of machinery and apparatus comes into view through reinforced glass.

- We just saw a lot of refraction at first, but there was definitely something else down there. Then it disappeared beneath the core, like a ghost. We've had positive readings of an unidentified object in numerous other sites across the grid.

Wakewater assesses the worker. He speaks with a detachedness that's disconcerting. Wakewater notes that all the riggers look the same; they all have fleecy facial hair and complexions of Nordic blusher. There's something about this planet, it produces identical native life forms. They have never been properly studied, these men of Terra. It has only ever been determined that they make fine workers. There hasn't been any detailed inquiry into their sense of empathy or how comparable their social and moral fabric is to humanoids on Earth. Are they even men? On the inside are they really men? Wakewater feels unsettled.

A helical screw is pummelling through the basin floor.

- Why are you still drilling? Stop it at once.

The bearded worker gives him a look that verges on irritation before signalling to the men in the control room to halt the machinery.

- What are you digging for? An apparition? This is a multi-national company dammit. My father started D-MON CORP from nothing, he won't have his money used in ridiculous covert excavations, of which you have no permission to complete by the way!

The bearded rigger frowns, all fear and respect is absent from his expression. Wakewater realises he is in the room alone with this man - his coxswain having opted to stay in the vessel. A fear creeps up on Wakewater, a fear he did not anticipate.

- You should know my name is Tarok, I run this operation.

Stunned by the gall of the man, Wakewater turns to leave back up the corridor. He gets about three steps into the shadowy, red lit hall when he sees a group of workmen blocking the path.

- This is my father's operation! No one else's! – Wakewater insists.

- There's been a change of plan.

- It took me four days to get to this planet. That includes a shuttle ride with no inflight meal and a rather violent boat trip with a chatty, Liverpudlian driver. I will not be treated like...

- You will be treated appropriately depending on your answer to the following question.

Wakewater stands, gap mouthed, waiting for the question.

- Do you believe in the Hearth?

Wakewater guffaws. He feels quite amused by how ridiculous the situation is fast becoming.

- The Hearth? Is this the same Hearth I'm thinking of?

- There is only one...

- This is ludicrous, the bloody *Hearth*?

Tarok steps forward so he's only inches away from Wakewater's face. Tarok smells of the sea, of potatoes and gin. There seems to be nothing going on behind his eyes. Tarok is a husk, a shell made in a maker's image.

- I can see the fear in you sir.

Wakewater does his best to disprove Tarok by staring confidently into his dead, cruel eyes.

- You will return to your father and tell him everything is fine. The Hearth is something we must find you see. We are certain that's what caused the lenses refraction. We have men dedicated to drilling for D-MON CORP, they know nothing of our other projects. You will not miss a few billion pounds funding or the small group of workers we have set aside in order to locate the Hearth.

- The Hearth isn't real!

- Then you do not believe?

- NO, I do not!

- This is unfortunate.

Tarok unbuttons his overall to the chest, revealing an inverted crucifix.

- As you can tell, I *do* believe…

Wakewater turns around to see the three workmen in the corridor exposing similar tattoos.

- You've all gone mad. I've heard too much time on the rigs can send a man insane. Take a holiday, please. We'll begin rotating more often…

- If you can't be persuaded to let us keep drilling, we can't let you leave sir.

- The Hearth isn't real. You believe the ghost of all consciousness is just wandering around the ocean of oil on Terra 5? I mean, that's just stupid!

- The Hearth is not a ghost. It is a spirit and the embodiment of all humanity, there's a difference.

Wakewater finds it ironic that this man should be so committed to the fabled God of human transubstantiation with eyes so hollow and awful.

- We have all been born on Terra 5, we grew up here. That the great Hearth should decide to roam our world is a blessing. We are surely chosen and unique.

Sensing the true extremity of danger he is now in, Wakewater Jr realises he must cooperate.

- Yes, I suppose you're right. Why else would you go to all this trouble?

This seems to satisfy Tarok, who buttons his overall back up.

- The people of Terra 5 will not have this blessing ruined Mr Wakewater. Our new spiritual mission has superseded your own. You understand?

- Of course.

Something strikes Wakewater about these beings – that they are obviously of limited intelligence. Beyond their natural grasp of basic labour, they cannot be trusted to perceive anything rationally. Only a delusional or grossly underdeveloped species would see a glimmer of light on a periscope and interpret it as God. A miniature cult on the Terra 5 oil platform is like something his father, Jacob Wakewater senior, would've rambled about in the height of his fever.

- Then you agree to be our conduit?

- Your conduit?

- The appendage through which the Hearth may communicate with his disciples.

Wakewater sees a strange reflection in the oil outside. The weather continues to thrash the tower with diagonal sheets of rain. Tarok is compelled to turn and gaze out the aperture into the vast black ocean of oil. Wakewater wonders if the same odd mote of light has ignited the superstition in Tarok.

- It is here. Right now, as we speak.

Tarok rubs his chin and through the grey mass of hair, a smile becomes visible.

- HE IS HERE! – Tarok punches the iron wall in an illustration of unbridled ecstasy. Wakewater looks out the aperture and now sees nothing. He disappears into the darkness.

The ripple of multi-coloured light is gone. In a strange way this somehow makes Tarok's beliefs more convincing. What was once there is now gone. And it was there, undoubtedly. Wakewater saw it with his own two eyes. Something deep inside the man has been moved. He finds himself yearning for another glimpse. When his will does not bring a re-occurrence, Wakewater is certain that he has witnessed the Hearth itself.

He can hear Tarok on the deck above, laughing like a jovial child in Earths warmest semester. Wakewater is determined to get to the above deck and see what Tarok sees. The three workers have remained in the corridor, preventing Wakewater from achieving his heart and souls desire.

- I beg of you Tarok, tell me what you see up there?

The rigger sighs audibly, triumphantly.

- The sight is magnificent. The seas have parted and turned a glorious blue. Waves of perfect white foam are crashing against the platform now.

- And the Hearth? You can see it?

He receives no answer.

YEAR OF THE COCKROACH

Originally published in Verbicide and Cadaverine

The sound of cocktail jazz in my ears rouses me back into wakefulness.

Lying cruciform on a table of Burmese glasses, a waitress stands beside me. It's a few moments before I feel the moisture on my fingertips and realise I'm knuckle-deep in her. She says something – I don't hear what. The electric fan on the ceiling is drowning everything else out. My faculties have been dulled by excessive whisky consumption. She dislodges me, moves away and my wet hand flops limply over the table.

I have felt the devils fingertips tickle the flesh around my ankles…

In 2061, the world is a pretty wondrous place and I, being a complete cynic, am keen to escape it. You don't have to tell me that my fate is a foregone conclusion.

I'm supposed to be a Time Detective but I'd be lying if I said I still had an ounce of passion left for the job. Travelling through the fabric of time and space every single day is the most laborious, draining, unrewarding job a guy could hope to land himself, believe me – this is from someone whose previous job was as a corpse handler during the last Syrian conflict.

Now don't get me wrong, there are people in this line of work who positively adore their job - take Deacon Fairfax for example. He thrives on dilation, on crossing dimensions and radically altering the curvatures of past and future time-scapes. You take Deacon Fairfax out of his job as a Time Detective however, and you're left with one boring ass motherfucker. I, on the other hand, am a man of numerous pleasures and past times. Who the hell wants to be transported to pre Krakatoa Indonesia, I mean really? Being a Time Detective only gets in the way of my true passion – being a full time drunken deadbeat. My name's Kip Novikov, I'm 46, divorced, bald and hopelessly addicted to all that's addictive. I do not appreciate atomising my time.

I always keep the standard issue gun handy. It can't hurt to have a photonic crystal machine capable of blasting wormholes in waterfront bars whenever an alcohol fuelled impulse to kill oneself comes crashing down – which they frequently do!

My Alert Watch goes off. I ignore it for as long as I can suffer the *bleep bleep bleeping* - then I answer it.

- NOVIKOV, MOSCOW 2015, 9:45PM, PALEONTOLOGY MUSEUM, NOW!

My scalp prickles with anger. I hate the little robotic voice telling me what to do all the time. I turn off the Alert Watch and keep my stare fixed on the burring fan blade above. Tucked into my belt is my photonic crystal gun. They want me to head to Russia but I can barely muster the motivation to lift my body from this table never mind get up, retrieve my gun, set the digits to the relevant time/location and push myself through a high velocity vortex. It's just too much sodding effort. Then something rises from below, my gut violently contacts – I need to puke.

In the bathroom the smell of urine is pungent, worsened by the malodorous air freshener fighting against it. Resting my chin on the filthy ceramic toilet bowl, the hot rust stink of blood hits me. In the murky toilet water I see my bile rich vomit run-through with arterial red. I'm no doctor but that's never a good sign…

Suddenly, a Detective appears with his chronovisor down. Even the most timid and travel weary of officers are void of any malaise behind the visor. It hides the eyes you see – those wet eyes, a balcony to the bloodless, un-kissed lips… It makes us all look the same, makes us look cool, calculated, efficient. None of us are any of said adjectives behind it all.

He drags me outside where the weather is bone-achingly cold. Knelt on the gale lashed sidewalk I spit out a gruel of blood and look up at the beleaguered Time Detective. I must look like a Muslim with his face smashed to the temple carpet worshipping Allah.

- What's this about?

His jaw line clenches, I just know that beneath the chronovisor is a stare completely divorced from reality.

- You're going to Moscow Novikov.

- Actually, I don't think I will be. Don't really fancy it, sorry.

He bites his bottom lip with a yellow, decayed incisor.

- You are going to Moscow.

- Listen… (I check his ID badge)…Stemson, I'm sure you're a great Detective. You look serious about the work and I can tell you're committed from that sex starved desperation oozing from every pore in your face, but if you could just do me this one favour and fuck off out of my sight, it'd be greatly appreciated.

- You ARE going to Moscow Novikov!

He cocks his photonic crystal gun and blasts a tear in the bar wall. He reaches down and seizes my collar with two industrial gloved bear paws.

- You need to go to Moscow Novikov.

With that, Stemson hurls me head-first through the wormhole. Looks like I'm going to Moscow…

****

A pair of snow glazed boots appear inches from my face. From the government insignia emblazoned on the hem of his pant leg, I know already I'm about to meet a Russian Time Detective – Moscow branch. Then a large hand, one which could clutch an entire calf skull in its palm, offers to help pull me up. All Russian TD's look the same. The chronovisor is more elaborate (it has to be to accommodate their large heads and effervescent facial hair). Being of Russian lineage myself, you'd think I could relate to these ambivalent Eastern chaps in the brutish head-gear. But as it happens, the only thing I've inherited from my Gram and pop-pop, Vlad and Greta Novikov, is their penchant for coma inducing premium standard vodka (Though, apparently Aunt Greta was once notorious for her wandering eye and frequent bed hopping - another habit I've become the heir to). I'm fairly British in most other respects – I attribute my cold sense of detachment to my mother's side of the family from Allison Street, Govan-hill. I dust myself off. Without warning, a booming Slavic accent emerges.

- Vadeneyev, Boromir - It's only when I see his massive index torpedo point to the name badge on his breast pocket that I realise he's telling me his name.

- Kip Novikov – I feebly point to my own weathered badge.

- You must come with me to the Palaeontology Museum to meet your contact.

An IRS sized headache is dawning. Vomit rises to my oesophagus and I choke it back down. The sourness stays on my tongue in a way which almost makes me cogitate about the state of my life.

- Right, right. Lead the way.

It occurs to me that I was born in 2015. The knowledge of this is as insignificant as my life is in 2061. It's the Chinese year of the wood sheep, whatever meaning that may have. Boromir and I trudge through 7 inches of snow towards Profsoyuznaya street. The alcohol has more or less worn off, at least subsided. The Russian air has a sobering effect on me. Our journey is silent but my strength is returning.

We approach the red sandstone building which looks less like a museum and more like an industrial factory. Plumes of smog gush out in a swirling maelstrom and I wonder what its source could possibly be. It's shocking to see the sheer dominance of Brutalist architecture in this country. Like Germany, Russia does little to banish their wretched reputation of being a truly humourless bunch.

- There is your contact.

I squint through the blizzard's haze and see a figure standing on the steps.

- Go to him. I must head back.

Boromir about-faces and begins stomping through the snow dunes in the opposite direction. My contact is a tall, slender man. He seems oddly familiar. The closer I get, the less distorted his physiognomy; that pale, stretched face, a little younger than I remember. That distinctly European smell of cucumber peels and strained tea. It's him. It's my grandfather…

- Grandpa Vlad?

- So this is what you look like as an adult?

He groans making no secret of his obvious disappointment.

- They told me you were a drunk and a phony. I thought they were just trying to make it easier for me.

- Easier to do what?

Grandpa Vlad is oblivious to the sense of bewilderment his words evoke. He brings out a long Russian cigarette and tries lighting it. The weather denies him his cigarette. The spark won't catch on his lighter and the dancing flame appears only for a brief second before disappearing in a single whisper. Frustrated, he puts the cigarette back in his pocket.

- Your father wanted nothing to do with this you know?

- To do with what? What's going on?

- In your time, a nuclear disaster is nigh, the explosion will destroy Earth.

- Ok…

- I am to blame in a way but more specifically you are to blame Kip.

- Me?

- You are the disruption to the non-linear system that triggers the eventual decimation of mankind.

Through the mist of confusion a more recognisable emotion surfaces – that of umbrage.

- That's a bit harsh!

- Chaos theory, *you* are the Cascading Failure Kip. When you travel back and forth through time you are reinforcing the cataclysmic flaw you embody. But the British branch of

TD's have given me this last opportunity to put things right. I had to be the one to do it in order to defeat the cycle.

- To do what?

The old man materialises a pistol from the depths of his trench coat. There's very little remorse on his face, which is disheartening I must say. I get a feeling which brinks on hopelessness, the strange indescribable pang put in motion by a family member's declaration of disappointment. A speed-bump forms in my epiglottis, if I wasn't such a "man" I could cry.

- How am I to blame? How can that possibly be my fault?

- The details were never clarified, all I know is the world gets blown to bits and it's all your bloody fault.

Grandpa says everything matter-of-factly, like an Islamic scholar declaring fatwa.

- Time travel was only made possible in 2038, that's 23 years away! How can you even be aware of any of it?

- I was visited. They thought I was crazy. When I told your grandmother about the time travelling detectives she almost left me. I've seen the future, they showed me.

- But Grandpa Vlad, I...

- You have to be here in 2015, the year of your conception, for this to work.

Grandfather raises the pistol to his head and pushes the nozzle hard at the temple. His finger squeezes over the trigger and the crack of fire echoes through the air. The old man drops to his knees then doubles over again to make a perfect snow angel on the alabaster pavement. I look at my hands expecting them to begin fading away, the Grandfather Paradox complete. But nothing happens. I'm still here. Then it hits me like an anvil from the top story of a High Rise.

Thank god for Aunt Greta's wandering eye...

I see a wormhole form and a team of Time Detectives with high powered government weaponry underarm. They've come for me. I start galloping through the thick snow, desperate to hold onto the pathetic excuse for a life I call my own. I may well be the lone component which sees our species doomed but I've never been so charged and motivated. How typical of me. Give me a long life on a plate and I'll crave death. Threaten to take my awful existence away for free at the expense of humankind's eventual saviour and I want to go on surviving...

BARJO AND HIS ALL-AMERICAN DRUGS

Originally featured on BizarroCast

ONE

Barjo's drugs tasted like shit. This didn't make them any less addictive. People got soul hungry for Barjo's gear, 10 times worse than your typical starving junky gets. They come in their droves to see him. People travel from miles around to Barjo's desert hut searching for his transcendental fix. His drugs gave the user a unique high. Some say it got you as close as safely possible to the orgasm of being hanged, when your neck snaps and that final measure of ejaculate starts running down your pant leg. Barjo attracted big customers who were dying to know his secret formula.

Barjo heard a knock on his wooden door, the frantic, desperate clawing common amongst hungry customers.

- Wait a sec.

Barjo unhooked the door and stuck out his head. He looked down at a sorry looking sap with a patchy white beard and wearing a red snowsuit. He was covered in desert sand that rested on his shoulders like dunes of dandruff. Barjo threw his arms out merrily.

- Come in, come in!

- Merry Christmas motherfucker.

- I'll scare up some tea!

Barjo welcomed his guest, giving a warm, firm handshake. He seemed pleased to see him, for Barjo knew the sap well - it was none other than old Saint Nick himself!

- Fucking weather. You need to start coming to me Barjo. The old man said gruffly, removing his hat. He immediately began rolling up his sleeves to reveal deep welt marks and collapsed veins gone gangrenous.

- You sure you're good to go Nick?

Santa Claus glared at Barjo as if to say – *Come on mother fucker, I know what I'm doing. I been doing this shit long before you were born, so get needling!*

Barjo pulled out a long hypodermic and tweaked the tip. It was already full of a murky substance, the contents of which remained mysterious. He found a vein cable travelling up the course of Santa's forearm and stuck in the tip. Santa gave a relaxed sigh as Barjo dropped the plunger. Both eyes rolled into the back of his skull as the liquid left the gauge and entered into his bloodstream. Santa rarely came anymore; his nerves were almost dead to the orgasm inducing properties of Barjo's drugs.

- It's almost Christmas. I need a hit just to fucking cope.

- I hear ya.

Barjo removed the needle and began dabbing at the area of blood. Santa looked grateful.

- I can get you extra perks Barjo. You've always been good to me. You got any kids who need anything, a Buzz Light-year or a Malibu Barbie doll or something?

- Nah. You sort of lose track of the seasons out here, you know?

- You really ought to think about relocating Barjo. I'm amazed you got any customers at all way out here in the middle of nowhere.

- I do ok. How you been coping? How's the missus?

Barjo went over to a drawer and brought out a metal money tin while waiting for a reply.

- Hah, that bitch can go to hell. One fucking word – alimony!

- I hear ya.

- Plus I got the Skid Row Spics and niggers after me. I'm owing some major doe-ray-me.

- What for this time?

Barjo put the money box on the table in front of Santa, who took the hint and put in a handful of 20's.

- I asked some favours and I gotta pay up. They threatened to cut off the head of my reindeer.

- That sucks Santa – he said with genuine sympathy in his voice. Barjo put the money tin back its drawer. Santa went on.

- I got this rogue elf called Jimmy see. He's been riling up the other workers, putting crazy ideas about trade unions in their heads. Now half of the little fucks won't work for less than 6 dollars an hour. Used to be, in the old days, you could get a decent elf labourer for a tub of Marys' homemade casserole. Those were the day's man. I'm three payments behind on my sleigh tax and I just don't know if I'm going to make it this year. They're threatening me with all kinds of legal shit. Pretty soon I might not be permitted to leave the state.

- The kids will forgive you Santa.

- Fuck the kids! I got my reputation to keep. Since the dawn of civilised society I never missed a round. Damned if I'm starting now.

Santa stared at the ground with a guilty expression.

- "I didn't mean that...about the kids I mean...I'm just tired.

Barjo placed a consolatory hand on Santa's shoulder.

T W O

Barjo's second customer arrived at the usual afternoon time. His customer was disarmingly effeminate and had large brown sunglasses which hid his junk wasted eyes. He had a gaunt Arab face and wore a plaid shirt unbuttoned to the chest like Jim Morrison. His expression suggested he'd twist the head off a puppy to score.

- Jesus Christ, the saviour! - Cried Barjo, embracing Jesus Christ the saviour. Behind Jesus, a long stretch limo was parked out on the ergs. The windows were blacked out but Barjo knew who it was inside. Jesus had the face of a dying dog on the vet table; he was noticeably hungry and impatient.

- My dad's insistent upon waiting for me. Shall we?

- Tell him to come in.

- No, I don't think that's a good idea Barjo. He's been in an utterly frightful mood of late. Please, let's get going.

- Fair enough I suppose.

Barjo fetched his money tin from the drawer and pulled out a syringe and Pyrex tube from a compact case. He drew a quota of the murky liquid into the syringe barrel and started tweaking. Jesus was wriggling in his seat, trying to suffocate an itch between his buttocks. He was a notoriously antsy customer and always had bugs under his skin. An air bubble collected at the nozzle and Barjo tutted then shrugged.

- Spose I don't need to worry about you getting an embolism.

Jesus smiled and pulled out his cock to find a vein for Barjo to inject. It was long and copper skinned and Barjo was used to injecting long time users in awkward places.

- Have you been reading your bible?

- I try - Barjo lied.

- I don't blame you. I'm misquoted like crazy in that damn thing.

They found a tumescent line to inject that ran down the seam of Jesus's penis. It was purple and only surfaced when teased with the tip of Barjo's needle. Jesus's heart rate began to spike. He stuck it in and pushed. Jesus clenched his sphincter tightly and a hot spring of semen shot forth into Barjo's face.

- Shit. I'm awful sorry man.

Barjo shook out a rag and wiped his face down, reassuring Jesus that it was no big deal.

- How's Damien?

Jesus smiled faintly, cock eyed with drug saturation.

- He's good. We tried for one of those civil marriages but, well, you know my dad.

- I do.

- Say Barjo, how come you're living rough in a dump like this? I thought with the money you rake in from peddling that miracle drug of yours, you'd be able afford a bigger joint?

- I'm a simple man Lord.

Jesus began fingering the stipe of his crucifix as his eye balls reeled. Barjo slid his metal money tin onto the table in front of the stoned Jesus and he dropped a fistful of crisp, green notes into it.

- Praise Jesus!

****

Barjo was kind of funny looking. He had strange yellowy flesh tone that bordered somewhere between Hispanic and Asian. His teeth could rip through tin. He had a ton of heavy piercings that hung like dangling chandeliers from his septum, ear lobes, brow and lower lip. Along his neck and arms there was always a weeping wound of some kind held together with paper stitches he'd obviously weaved himself. This gave him the appearance of a monster poorly assembled by a mad scientist. Barjo was balding too but the hair he did have ran round either side of his head to meet in a Kimbo Slice beard the colour of Orc blood. Despite being rakishly skinny with no definable musculature, Barjo was deceptively strong (which is why no one fucked with him). Strangest of all, Barjo was totally Buddhist and, while he could give most hard-up junkies an ass kicking, he'd rather keep his business clean (which is why everyone respected him). His accent was also difficult to pin down. It occasionally emerged in lazy S lisps like a Spaniard but he burred his R's like a Scotsman. People doubted if Barjo was even a human being at all.

****

There was a third loud chap at Barjo's door that evening. He hadn't been expecting anyone till midnight. Keeping this in mind, Barjo opted to check through his peephole before letting anyone in straight away. He saw two Caucasian men wearing business suites and carrying Samsonite briefcases. They peered over the rim of expensive Oakley sunglasses and adjusted the Windsor knot of their ties in perfect synch. Barjo opened the door and both faces animated long, phony Cheshire grins.
- Mr Barjo?
- The same.
- May we come in.
- Depends.
- Please sir, we're good people.
The suit said this robotically thus failing to dispel Barjo's reticence. The stink of hair lacquer and cologne hovered above the men like a raincloud of important smell. Barjo reluctantly stood aside to allow the men entry. He noticed slight dissimilarities between them. One wore a black single breasted suit, strongly padded at the shoulders (Suit 1) and the other wore a double breasted seersucker, which owed more to midnight blue than black (Suit 2). Barjo apologised for the odd smell that hung around in the hut (referring to the sharp salty aroma of his client's semen). Barjo asked the fellas if they wanted a drink. They both declined. Suit 1 folded his arms and said sternly,
- It's come to our attention Mr Barjo that you've been supplying a highly toxic substance illegally?
Barjo gave a theatrical groan.
- You're FDA huh?
Suit 2 put both hands up in mock surrender and began reassuring Barjo in a soft, polite accent.
- On the contrary Mr Barjo we've come here with a proposal.
They had the good cop/bad cop routine to a tee – Suit 1 was the impatient bully and Suit 2 the more compassionate, by-the-book character.
- What kind of proposal?
- The business kind Mr Barjo.
- I don't understand.
Of course, Barjo understood perfectly. He tried to stop himself from smiling victoriously.
- We want to buy your drug Mr Barjo.
- Buy me out eh?
- Yes. We work for Chen Multinational. We just need a sheet of ingredients and these briefcases full of $100 bills are yours.
- Trouble is I can't tell you that.

Suit 2 motioned forward a little.

- Please Mr Barjo, be reasonable. We've got enough money for you to get out of this seedy dealer lifestyle and start afresh.

- I make plenty of money. I choose to live this way.

- There's been speculation as to the key properties of your drug Mr Barjo. Suit 1 said in a no-bullshit sort of way. Barjo went over to his window and drew the curtain.

- What've you heard?

- We heard lots of things - goats cum, dragon urine, God nectar, all manner of mystical faeces and plasma, and all speculation of course.

The suit held his stare on Barjo to clarify that it wasn't in fact any of the things he'd just mentioned.

- No. It's none of that shit.

- I'm paraphrasing obviously.

Suit 1 brought out a ream of paper and started reading from it.

- Your drug also seems to change etymology. We've heard it called Jam Cap, Tusk, Divine Firecracker, Acid Wank, and The Long Slow Orgasm!

Suit 1 got real close and Barjo could smell corporate dick on his breath.

- We can make you wealthy sir.

Normal people couldn't afford to keep up the habit and still support themselves financially. This is why Barjo's main clientele are all of high celebrity status. What these two goons couldn't seem to realise was that he didn't need their money.

- Sorry guys, but I'm gonna have to ask you both to scoot.

- Excuse me? Said Suit 1 indignantly.

- I got a customer coming soon and I gotta prime up his needle. And anyway, the pails need to be mucked out .

- *Excuse me*? Said Suit 1 and Suit 2 in chorus.

Barjo gestured to several steel pails brimming over with spunk. Suite 1's hand automatically went up to his mouth. Suit 2 stifled a strong gag then both men left.

THREE

JFK's tongue flopped out of his mouth like a wet fish as he felt Barjo's drug brush over blunt sensory receptors.

- Holy shit, I can see through time…

- Ok John.

Kennedy was dramatic. Barjo humoured him. Barjo withdrew the needle spike and dabbed at the pinprick. JFK never came; he was unique in that respect. In fact, he had a different biological response to the drug entirely. Rather than kindle arousal in him, it acted more like a psychedelic. JFK claimed he could see the fabric of the universe and often described to Barjo, in great detail, the scale of hallucinations he experienced. Barjo knew why JFK's response was different from his other clients. The hole in the ex-president's head wiped out all his neurotransmitters, deactivating the area of the brain stem responsible for sexual stimulation. God bless old Lee Oswald. Then JFK started coughing and spluttering.

- Fuck, I'm getting the horrors man...
- Try and relax John.

But the former president was already doubled over and vomiting up green bile. When he brought his head back up his eyes were buckshot and hysterical. Streams of drool wetted his chin and he began hyperventilating and grabbing at Barjo's shirt.

- John, you ok?

JFK couldn't answer - his mouth was too full of slobber and vomit and choked tears. The hole in the back of his head began leaking brain juice and it took an almighty slap from Barjo to calm JFK down. The slap was so hard and violent that the resulting CRACK echoed a little and nearly knocked the president's brain right out of his skull.

- Thanks man...

JFK pulled himself back up onto the seat. Barjo went over to collect his money tin, checking back on his customer, relieved to see a controlled fear in him. From here JFK's face looked kind of odd. He had these dull eyes like a crustacean and he rarely blinked to moisten them. JFK really seemed to be staring through time...

****

Barjo opened the hatch door leading into the basement and made his way downstairs. He tugged at a ceiling light cord and the bulb fired into life. Standing in front of him was a dimly-lit naked figure hooked up to all kinds of apparatus. You could see his heart beating behind the chest he was so thin. Wires and tubes ran in and out of every orifice draining all fluid from his body and into a large plastic blood bag. Barjo went over and collected the bags that were full and began straining them into Pyrex tubes. The poor individual wore only a large top hat with stars and stripes on it and was bound to the wall with metal fasteners. He tried to talk but before he could utter a sound, Barjo shoved a tequila bottle into his mouth and forced its contents down his throat. Tequila ran all down his face and beard. Underneath the top hat, the man's skull had been balled like a melon with most of the brain scooped right out. His eyes were moist with tears, unable to express his long unnecessary pain.

- Hey Sam you trying to communicate?

Barjo's prisoner mumbled unintelligibly, dribbling saliva and tequila.

- Schadenfreude Sam...

Barjo smiled and went back upstairs to cook his drug.

GENE RESURRECTED

ONE

Gene held on tight to the support bar. The train hurtled through its tunnel and the whole carriage shook like crazy. Subways were kind of like purgatory. You're stuck between places. Between A and B. Gene's life was spent in subway dawns. In purgatory.

Across from Gene was a rough looking mother fucker with a dog eared jacket worn to thread at the elbows and he must've been a hobo or a junkie or a fag (or all three!), because there was desperate hunger in his drawn, ill face. He only had one shoe on where the fattest toe poked out front and wriggled around on occasion. The mother fuckers face was like a golem mask, pock marked with bushy eyebrows that hid his stare a little. He was looking straight at Gene. His teeth were rotted into his head and when he smiled they showed through like a lemon rind gum-shield. Gene pretended not to see. He felt uncomfortable being ogled like this. He was to become more uncomfortable as the mother fucker began mouthing the words I'M GOING TO FUCK YOUR TIGHT LITTLE ASSHOLE from across the cart. A passenger next to Gene reading the sports pages caught the mother fucker doing this, only to return casually to his paper. The mother fucker pulled his hand up to his mouth and began licking the index finger, rolling it in and out of his mouth in an obvious effort to seem sexual. Then he made an O with his finger and thumb and started shoving his tongue through the hole suggesting all sorts of sick activity. Gene dropped his gaze to his own shoes. They were finely polished until a wad of spit landed on the eyelet and dribbled over the leather. The spit wad came from the mother fucker's direction and Gene's mind started throwing up panic signals about aids and hepatitis when he noticed the drool run through with sick yellow and faint traces of blood. Gene couldn't resist making eye contact. When he looked up, the mother fucker was making loud coughing noises with no attempt to cover his mouth as large gobbets of infected sputum flew around the entire carriage. A kid wearing a Throbbing Gristle sleeveless t-shirt smirked and leaned against one of the support poles. In the crowded cart, the smells of sweat and farts tainted the air in a way which seemed to totally compliment the lecherous mother fucker that was propositioning Gene. The train rattled fiercely until it came to a screeching halt on the tracks outside the main platform. Gene prayed the creep got off soon. Three stops later he realised the motherfucker was here for the long haul, probably waiting for Gene to get off so he could follow him and rape him in an alley. A kid changed sides on his thrift store cassette player.

The week hadn't been a good one. His boss at the denim factory pretty much told him he'd be one of the first shit canned in the next downsize. Gene wouldn't miss the factory work but he was 2 payments behind on the rent and Mr Mendoza, the landlord, was getting touchy (it was a bad idea to piss Mendoza off because word on the street is he's an ex Latin King Gang leader). Gene's girlfriend left him the week before because she got a job working for some cock sucker with connections in channel 7, Detroit. Susie was always kind of too pretty for a guy like Gene anyway. On top of that his dad died after a 4 year battle with anal cancer. Gene's health was deteriorating at a sobering rate. Bad posture has given him the crooked spine of an 80 year old when Gene was only 25. He suffered from hypotension, obesity, IBS, insomnia and he hadn't been to the dentist since he was like 12, so he had toothache 24/7 and was told on more than one occasion that his breath smelled like an asshole. He was also impotent and socially awkward, which he attributes to Susie eventually leaving him, but it could've been a culmination of numerous flaws that proved the deal-breaker. Life seemed like a cruel, fucked up joke and he was the punch-line. He'd thought about suicide, of course he'd thought about it! But he always kind of woosed out at the final push. He had excuses to fall back on then - responsibilities to his parents, his girlfriend…but now pretty much all of those things had gone and abandoned him and Gene honestly just didn't give a fuck anymore.

The train pulled into the terminal - last stop. Gene tried to squeeze in his gut to escape the motherfucker and lose himself in the crowded cart, but Gene's gut only got so flat before he had to exhale again. The motherfucker's eyes stayed right on him. Gene felt a tug at his tie, pulling him into the crush of passengers, like Jaws dragging a dumb surfer under the water by his leg. He was relieved to see a woman's face on the end of it. She had cute features and a tight figure. Her hair had been pulled back and she wore hooped earrings that jangled in musical collaboration with the bracelets around her wrist. Her face was young and kind. Gene did not know this woman.

- Tito Mendoza? She said, smiling faintly up at Gene.
- Um…Mr Mendoza my landlord?

The woman stood up so she was facing him now. Gene caught her perfume which smelled of freshness and modernity. The train passengers continued to pour out of the carriage. The motherfucker also appeared to have taken the hint and made like a tree. Gene felt his spirits rejuvenated already as he flirted with this beautiful stranger who somehow knew his landlord.

- You know Mr Mendoza?
- Uh huh, he my fuck'n unc yo…
- Excuse me?

The girls faced ceased its kind delicacy. Her skin scrunched into leathery wrinkles and raw hate was her only definable trait. Then there was a sudden flashing image of two oncoming fists landing on Gene's right temple. BANG – BANG! Gene hit the floor, more out of shock than actual force.

- He wants his fuck'n money dog! Squealed the woman as she flung her purse over one shoulder and exited the subway.

Walking past the 42nd street movie theatre the whole city seemed to scream in Gene's face – the traffic, the people, the cops dunking their donuts into pots of hot coffee, the kids hurdling skip ropes, the flashing signs, the hustlers picking up new product outside the Disney store and the poodles fucking in the heat. Gene couldn't face going home to an empty apartment. Susie had taken most of the CD's and electrical appliances when she left. He felt burdened by all his losses. Most of the shit that went down was 100% Gene's own doing. He couldn't provide for Susie. All he had to offer the woman he loved was a one bedroom apartment in a crumby neighbourhood. Gene was grossly out of shape too. His three a day consisted of Jolly Rancher candy bars, Mentos, strawberry shakes from Burger King or cherry flavoured soda. He ate sticks of jerky like they were chips from the bag. Gene never exercised and drank liquor way too often to ever be casual about it. He smoked cigarettes and joints and when he wasn't pressing denim, he was sitting on his fat, lazy ass all day watching reruns of M.A.S.H. No wonder Susie bailed when she did. So you've pretty much gathered that Gene is a complete loser.

Gene stuck his key into the lock half expecting Mendoza to have switched them over, but to his relief the key still worked – for now at least. Thoughts of suicide had already begun to resurface by the time Gene collapsed onto the sofa and saw that the only thing on was Dr Phil or Roseanne. He lit up a joint and dozed off wearing the clothes he'd worn to work that day. He drank a bottle of whisky beforehand and woke up the next morning with piss stains all down the crotch of his pants.

TWO

On the subway the next day the motherfucker was back, only this time he had a freshly pressed Stetson suit on. Gene found that he was the one doing most of the staring now. No matter how hard Gene tried to make eye contact with the smart dressed motherfucker, he just couldn't catch any. It was almost like the motherfucker who'd wanted to rape him so bad yesterday were embarrassed by the obvious gapes Gene was giving. The train screeched into the terminal. The motherfucker picked up his briefcase and hurried out of the train.

Walking back through 42nd street Gene was filled with an overwhelming feeling of woe, more significant than that of yesterday. It felt more significant because, while the same hopelessness and agony remained, a heavy tedium had snuck up on Gene wringing out the last drop of life in him. This city was so fucked up. Gene's dad once told him - a city that lacks the fear of death is a man after my own heart - Whatever that means? Sometimes you gotta destroy the town to save it. Gene walked under the tall stone legs with windows punched in at the knee cap and watched tongues of tarmac taking cars to and from its hub like lambs catching sight of the slaughterhouse unit, the virus entering its host - Conveyor belts of homunculi cased behind peanut shells of metal

He got to the front steps of his apartment and saw the door caved in. There were hand prints of blood streaked across the window that continued along the hallway inside. A woman's dress and underwear lay in a wet bundle on the reception desk. Gene could hear women screaming and the cutting clamour of Mr Mendoza laughing maniacally. Gene got the hell out of there.

He wandered to the store where some kids hustled him for a light. When he said he didn't have one (which he did), they stole his pants and took it anyway. A guy who looked a little like Jesus Christ marched through the streets wearing a loin cloth, a crown of bloodied thorns and carrying a huge crucifix across his shoulders told Gene he was going to hell and no one would care when he was dead. What a prophet!

On his last legs now, Gene could only think of alcohol because he was unable to get into his apartment for any joints. Standing in his off-yellow, polka-dotted underpants in the middle of Harlem, you see that Gene wasn't exactly a streetwise kind of guy. He could hear the sound of gushing water and was drawn to it like a kid following an ice cream truck jingle. When he got to its source, the river that separated Manhattan from the Bronx burbled and flowed and Gene was now standing on the edge of 3rd Avenue looking down at the grey waves. Southbound traffic hurtled by from East 135th street. He took a deep breath and pulled himself to the girder. Gene waited a moment to see if any of the passers-by or tourists tried to stop him.

- I'm gonna jump…

When he realised they weren't listening, he jumped…

In hell, Gene opened his eyes to see a familiar face inches from his own – David Letterman. He wore a really nice sweater and tamped out ash from a huge Corona. He looked like he always did with those round bifocals, buckteeth and that silver ledge of hair. But on closer inspection Gene noticed scales like a lizard, you had to look real close to see them they were so well hidden. Letterman pulled his enormous reptilian head away from Gene and offered him a hand up. Each finger was adorned with large 24 carrot sovereigns and doubloons. Gene reached for Letterman's hand and upon contact felt that his skin was nothing like that of a human being either. It felt clammy or cold somehow, not exactly the state of circulation you'd expect to find in the subterraneous depths of hell. Once on his feet, Gene observed the flamethrowers tossing up clouds of fire and the lake of blood running between Letterman's throne and he knew this was hell. Johnny Carson kneeled beside him asking if he wanted any shit cleaned up. Letterman just grinned, poised his ass over Carson and began making straining noises. When the deed was done, he began rubbing Carson behind the ears. N'Sync were doing a dance routine while miming at the same time, Barry Manilow sang repeated choruses from Mandy. Dwarf orgies were happening everywhere, so too were interracial gangbangs between politicians and pro-wrestlers. There was a row of 10 doors like the ones you get in a cheap speakeasy motel, each one numbered. Behind each door came an awful howling.

- EEEUUURRRGGGHHHH-FUCKIN-ARRRGGGHHH-AARRRGGGHHH!

Letterman smirked at Gene and pulled a rod of bone from the lake of blood that'd been carved into the shape of an Emmy award.

- I'M YOUR OVERLORD MAGGOT. NOW AIN'T YOUR TIME. SO GET THE FUCK BACK UP THERE. HANG ONTO YOUR WIGS AND KEYS!

With that, Letterman struck Gene on the skull with the bone and he dropped to the gravel.

THREE

Gene woke up rubbing his head. A lump had already begun to form the size of walnut. He was in a strange mansion somewhere and he had no idea how he got there. The wallpaper was pinstriped red and white which didn't in any way compliment the cowhide shag. A poodle barked outside from a doghouse somewhere. He remembered the hot smell of cigar smoke on Letterman's breath and the rest was too vague to recall in any great detail. The surface he was lying on belonged to a king size mattress and it was so comfortable he had difficulty getting out of bed. Gene stretched and looked around the room. It was huge, like Hefner huge. Above the bed was a huge wooden shelf groaning under the weight of several philosophy and style books. In the chest of drawers (which he somehow knew was a flea-market find) were dozens of wallet-sized condom tabs. Gene unwrapped one and began massaging the rubber sheath like a plush water snake. He went over to the silvered mirror and couldn't believe what stared back at him. Gene's body had changed. Somehow his suicide had brought with it superior health. He was barrel chested for Christ sake. Gene was broad shouldered too, he'd never been broad shouldered before; his arms and legs pulsed with powerful mounds of muscle. His stomach was divided into a pack of 6 and Gene saw that in his off-yellow, polka-dot underpants was a penis he didn't recognise either. It was fucking huge, throbbing and purple and fat. This all felt like some sort of beautiful dream, until he noticed his face. Prior to all this, the one part of Gene he found least fault with was his face. His body went to shit sure, but his face was never too bad. It was considered Gene's saving grace. If it weren't for his face he would've NEVER gotten laid. Not that Gene's face was *all that* but you get the picture, in comparison with the rest of his body Gene's face came off like fucking Brad Pitt. But now it was different. While his body advanced, the face seemed distorted. It was like Gene had one of those old Scream masks on. He felt his heart begin to race and his belly twisting in weird ways at the sight of himself. Then he relaxed. He observed his body in profile and felt a little better. Gene realised he no longer had his taste for weed and whisky.

There was a knock at the door. He tried to say "Come in" but was unable to move his mouth. The door turned and a girl walked in. She was great looking. Her hair was long and blonde and she wore a tube top that pushed her breasts up just below her chin.

- You want to fuck me? The blonde girl said in a broken English accent. Gene nodded because that's all he could do from the neck up.

- Call me motherfucker. She whispered

She strolled over to him and kicked off her heels. She started playing with Gene's new-improved horse dick and he forgot all about the disfigured appearance of his face. Gene could hardly remember the last time he'd felt this happy.

- You're a BIG boy aren't ya? The girl teased, flicking her tongue against the helmet. He was approaching a climax seconds into it (Gene never was a very good, lasting lover) and threw one of his huge, beefy hands onto the hot blondes shoulders to steady himself. He pushed her down to groin level. Gene wanted to scream I'M COMING! I'M COMING YOU MOTHERFUCKER as he felt the measure of cum make the long journey from his balls to the tip of his penis head. Gene's cock fired out a round like a pump action shotgun into the girls face, hard, fast and through the other side of her head. When Gene opened his eyes he saw the headless blonde kneeling, still clutching onto the shaft of his penis. The room was awash with blood and spunk and Gene saw that his load had fired straight through the girl and left a gigantic hole in the wall. He wanted to thank David Letterman, praise the lord! He wanted to shout I'M NOT A LOSER! I JUST BLEW A CHICKS HEAD OFF WITH MY FUCKIN' SPUNK BULLET...but, of course, he couldn't. Suicide had made him super virile. He thanked the good lord David Letterman for this second chance at living life. Fuck Susie, fuck Mr Mendoza. Gene went to the window and drew back the curtain. It was a beautiful New York day outside. Suicide had granted him a new upstate mansion too. He didn't know if he was alive or dead, he didn't care either. All Gene knew was that he liked things much better this way. He put the blonde girl's body into the laundry chute and went downstairs.

He switched on the huge widescreen TV and dropped himself onto the Ikea egg chair. He opened a carton of orange juice which wound up spilt all over his face. M.A.S.H was on but he felt his brain required more than it was able to deliver. Something in him desired an intellectual challenge. He did the crossword puzzle in less than 30 seconds with an extra 10 seconds for the Brainteaser at the end (the answer was Tito Puente). Gene was a perfect specimen of male physicality, sexuality and intellectuality, all that was missing was the ability to fly. He got to wondering, could he fly? Gene drew back the curtains and stood up on the ledge. Flashbacks about his suicide jump in Harlem tickled the nape of his neck with déjàvu. He felt pretty certain he could fly. Gene was more or less a fucking superhero. His confidence was on such a high there wasn't anything he doubted he could do. The balls of his heel rolled on the ledge rail. Gene stuck out both hands like an Olympic swimmer and took in another deep breath. He leapt forward, cutting the air with his face. Gene fell 10 stories and onto the pavement.

Turns out he couldn't fly…

PIG-FACE CHRISTUS WE HARDLY KNEW YEE

The priest dawned his vestigial robe and observed the Vitruvian angles of the crucified girl. She was savagely thin, starved for an entire day in an act of imposed ritualistic abstinence – certainly she appeared a poor looking girl to the untamed eye.

A chorus of Gregorian chants suddenly groaned into life.

Priest Prelati was a surly chap who had actually been defrocked by the ecclesiastical authorities a few years before when news of his occult interests found public circulation. But in the wake of this virginal, delicate creature a perverse joy had overcome him. The leathery flesh around his mouth pulled tight into a sinister, triumphant smile.

- 'Finally I've found you. It took an age, but I've finally found you.'

Prelati had chased her for the longest time; through the ramparts of district Paris across the countries aire-urbane and even into Basque territory. In this time the girl's physical form had taken numerous permutations, first as a hare, then a drake, then as a greyhound. Beneath the layers of subcutaneous fat, the serpent lay in hiding – in its true form, the body free of manifestation that slithered into our mortal realm through a crack in quantum hell.

The girl moaned again, her breasts undulating beneath her trembling chin. She had a bird-like beauty, bright, soft of feature, small hipped. Her face was a portrait of pure agony - an otherworldly adversary for Prelati to contend. He stifled a destructive arousal within himself. Having ceased her tormented moans, the girl began to speak, though her voice emerged in the growling thunder of a hell-dwelling demon.

> And bled and raped was I
> And scared was and cold was I
> Hey ho the noddy oh
> Hey ho the noddy oh
> Hey ho the noddy oh
> In fields of rape I lie

A trio of hooded figures observed from the chancel. There was a man of distinct residue in the middle. Guivarch was his name. Once a soldier during the Franco-Prussian war, in a previous incarnation he'd been a prolific child murderer. Now his efforts were solely devoted to worshipping the beast. For most of his formative years he had been plagued by horrifying images of a pig-faced man. He accredited these visitations as a key factor in the warping of his young mind.

- 'My God, what the hell's the matter with her?' – Guivarch whispered for fear of disturbing her recital.

- 'She's gestating.' - Said the priest elatedly - 'It won't be long till the serpent has to leave this body behind.'

- 'She looks in a state of deep trauma.'

'The serpent can see through the fabric of our universe, and beyond even that. She has vision which sees every possibility, past and present; a quite awful affliction. You'd look that way yourself in her position.'

- 'Can she contact the beast?'

- 'I certainly hope so. If anyone can see him, it'll be this doleful creature writhing before us.'

- 'So how long do we have?'

- 'Not long, the metatron can only last a few days in each host. Once the serpent is loose, it's no use to us. She's too powerful, too full of speed and resistance. If we're to obtain anything from her we need to act fast.'

Guivarch had a guilty face. This might suggest he felt some remorse for the hideous crimes he'd committed, but in truth his anxiety had more to do with a fear of his own execution than quiet lamentation.

Following the War of the Breton Succession, Guivarch earned the favour of the Duke and was admitted to the French court.

Both he and Prelati had amassed a decent amount of power and wealth, providing a perfect veil for their insidious pastimes.

- 'Fetch me the necromancer.'

Guivarch gestured to the hooded man resting in the choir stall. He drew his cowl and revealed himself to be Crowley. His face was unnaturally fresh as if he had access to a fountain of imperial youth.

It was initially the promise of pure Parisian opiates which had influenced his decision to travel all the way from Cambridge, but now, seeing the girl possessed by the metatron, Crowley had come to be freshly excited by the situation.

- 'If you'll indulge me for a moment gentlemen.'

He took out a syringe full to the dropper with Ottoman morphine. He pricked the hook of his arm and descended the plunger. Crowley sighed as a wave of spiritual energy ran a course from the base of his spine to the third cycloptic eye buried in the centre of his skull.

- 'Let's begin.'

Crowley snapped his fingers and an orphan boy ran to the stage. The boy was pulled in straight from the streets, that much was clear - an urchin, and when he stood before Crowley he bowed his head in chagrin. Guivarch saw the boy scuttle up the steps and restrained his base urge to harm him.

The boy stood shivering before the naked, possessed girl. Crowley took a step back and leaned in to priest Prelati.

- 'If this is the metatron, she will speak only to a pure blood. The serpent does not fraternise with sickness of the soul' – He gave a glance over to Guivarch as if to illustrate his point. The men watched as the urchin inched closer to the crucified girl. They seemed to exchange brief, almost silent dialogue before the boy reversed himself away from her. Crowley knelt to the boy's level. The boy cupped his hand around Crowley's ear and began revealing the words he'd shared with the serpent. Crowley's face was a combination of drug saturation and abject disappointment.

- 'I'm sorry gentlemen, but this creature is not what you believe it to be.'

- 'Excuse me?' – The priest spat indignantly.
- 'The creature. It isn't the serpent.'
- 'Well what the fuck is it then?'
- 'It seems to me to be more like a pig.'

Guivarch froze. Something profoundly affecting had just occurred to him.

- 'What's wrong with him?'
- 'I haven't the faintest idea?'

Guivarch stood mesmerised in shock, staring at the girl's distorted face. To his horror, the delicate features of this human female body were beginning to change.

- 'I can see its snout! Jesus…' – cried the former killer. Guivarch ran straight down the main aisle and out the door.

Prelati and Crowley followed him.

****

Outside, they found Guivarch slumped against the wall weeping.

- 'The guilt, this terrible guilt has finally caught up on me.'

Prelati was confused but Crowley seemed less surprised by this behaviour.

- 'What are you talking about?'
- 'God, that girl, the urchin child, I…'

Guivarch choked on his sorrow and could not utter the shameful truth.

- 'What??'
- 'I have killed them both before. Those children in there, I have killed them dead and now they are alive somehow. This is surely punishment!'
- 'Guivarch, you are delirious please get a hold of yourself!'
- 'This must be hell. My quest has finally reached its destination. All this time I had been so blind to it. I am the serpent don't you see, not the girl in there - ME!'
- 'We are so close, you must control yourself! We have precious little time for this.'
- 'I see all the ghastly shapes I have cast upon the world. I've never experienced a shred of remorse until now. I was driven by something, something not purely me, put on a path by some malevolent force, possessed by the serpent to bring me here - the site of my judgment.'

Guivarch broke down again. Prelati looked at Crowley's expressionless face.

- 'Fucking leave him.'
- 'But…'
- 'A man with such weight on his conscious is no good to us. We need focus, not distraction. If you want your demon to talk then leave him.'
- 'Very well, let's leave him…'

And so they did…

****

When the two men returned to the church the girl was gone, leaving behind an empty, blood blotched iron cross. The boy was gone also, as were the three hooded onlookers. The entire alter space was awash with viscera and vital organs, like someone had just been ploughed down by an invisible freight train. Scrawled almost illegibly across the clerestory was 'HAPPY

BIRTHDAY CHRISTUS?'
- 'I don't understand…' – Prelati confessed.
- 'You were too late. She's gone.'
- 'But…we were so close.'
Crowley sat on a pew and allowed the remainder of his heroin high to do its business.
- 'It would've ultimately been a fruitless effort anyway.'
- 'How so?'
- Because the creature presented itself to you for one reason.'
- 'And that was?'
- 'To burn an impression of your face onto its mind's eye so that it may never forget you. This pig-faced creature will haunt you until the day you die father.'
- 'I've spent the best part of my life trying to catch the fucking thing!'
- 'Maybe it really was after your mate out there, the child killer?'
- 'He is not a child killer.'
- 'He most definitely is father. I'm not here to judge, but it's written all over him. His soul stinks of a stagnant past.'
- 'I really thought I was going to communicate with the master.'
- 'There are consequences of a pursuit like that and I don't think you or your pal out there are up to dealing with that burden.'
Prelati looked at the hoof prints in the puddle of blood below his feet.
- 'A bloody pig eh?'
A scream came from outside…

PROTEUS

You cannot describe the heavy silence that hangs inside the Proteus's chamber...

He can no longer remember his own name...

The professors sentencing is tomorrow, when exactly he does not know.

Probably it will take place sometime after Lord Zinnia's circumcision. That said, Zinnia may wish to get the professor's trial over and done with so he can spend the rest of the day better preparing for the complicated surgery that lay ahead - times also being of the essence in the collapsing ergo-sphere.

It's difficult to be certain.

One thing is certain however – tomorrow, the professor will be executed. His only hope is to somehow break free - but escape is impossible from the constant dimensional shifts of the Proteus.

He'd been incarcerated within its walls following his part in a clandestine medical operation caught out by royal guards while trying to reveal the true secrets behind Proteus's seemingly autonomous nature. The closest they came to any answers lay in a codex filed away deep in the royal cabinet. The document gave details of a deity who constructed a confinement complex so isolating its prisoners would either turn over to justice or turn to suicide. The professor was consumed by its mystery.

Now, here he is, trapped inside the very facility he'd dedicated his research to uncovering - Lord Zinnia is a massive fan of ironic punishment.

The professor had begun to age rapidly. He figured it was something to do with the intensity of the region of space, the heaving vacuum of the black hole and the throbbing mind of the Proteus combining to destroy time.

His beard had already grown long and grey and cables of veins surfaced beneath his weathered flesh like railroad sleepers. His lips were cracked and his mouth unable to produce saliva. The professor was not an evil man. This complex was designed for intergalactic mercenaries and terrorists; all the professor could be accused of was giving into dangerous curiosity.

Proteus would only ever preserve its current function as a temporary detainment unit that sent men mad before their sentencing. If someone were to be kept inside for too long its structure becomes volatile, stretching and expanding the very composition of the universe itself.

What was, and remains, most curious about Proteus is that the entire block seems to be a naturally occurring phenomenon. No one has ever taken credit for building it and no blue print designs were ever found to explain the layout of its unique, complicated inner structure.

The Proteus architect is something else entirely.

****

The professor can't sleep. It's the relentless screams of the other prisoners rebounding off the steel walls around him that make rest impossible. Suspended in the zero-gravity of his chamber, he can only stare madly at the grotesque images the Proteus complex conjures up for him. For a while, it was the hovering body of his deceased wife that haunted him. But her face soon began changing into something much worse – a recurrent image of his daughter being brutally raped and murdered. It has become too much to bare. The professor screams and spits and tries clawing his own eyes out, but even after he manages to partially blind himself, the image has already been burnt into his mind. He feels his brain begin to leak out of his ears.

There is no escaping.

It feels like days but the professor has only been in isolation for a few hours. Even in this brief period, his mind has begun to unravel. Lord Zinnia is a selfish ruler but he is not without his mercies. Every two hours the professor's chamber is filled with an agent designed to numb the trauma of the visions. Lord Zinnia calls it "Respite". The professor has already received his first dose and simply cannot wait to get his next one.

All around him the floating prison begins to creak. By this stage of course the professor has lost his ability to differentiate between what the Proteus creates and what his own mind creates as a distress response. Perhaps the parameters of his mind are collapsing in on themselves.

When he opens his eyes, a blurred figure is hovering directly in front of him – a figure he does not recognise. The professor stays fixed on the vague apparition. He's trapped by a curiosity that sucks him in as if his tie were caught in the conveyor belt of some lethal machinery. A voice suddenly emerges, echoing around the chamber.

- I AM PAL

The professor's mouth is full of pause. He looks to his wrist and the tight shackles that once bound him to the steel border are gone.

- I AM A DIRECT MANIFESTATION OF THE PROTEUS.

- So…do you really exist?

- THE PROTEUS EXISTS THEREFOR I EXIST.

The figure's impression grew no clearer, even when the professor screwed up his eyes to narrow slits he couldn't see beyond the fog.

- Why have you chosen to appear in my presence?

- I APPEAR TO EVERY PRISONER OF THE PROTEUS.

- Are you the architect?

- NO

- Then who is?

- …YOU ARE.

The professor feels something in his gut fall on its side. He's startled back into effect by the tormented moans coming from the opposite chamber.

- I'm afraid you're mistaken.

- I'M AFRIAD IT IS YOU WHO IS MISTAKEN.

- I've spent my life living in the shadow of the Proteus's mystery. I've given my best years trying to understand it. I certainly didn't build the thing! Its structure is far too intricate and complex…

- YOU UNDERSTAND NOTHING OF WHAT I'M TRYING TO COMMUNICATE.

- You're right PAL, you're right!

- I'M SORRY YOU DO NOT UNDERSTAND

The professor makes a stark realisation about PAL.

- I know what you are you know?

- I SENSE THAT YOU DO NOT.

- You're either an illusion of the Proteus or a side effect of the "Respite". Whichever you may be, you remain a figment of my imagination.

- I'M MORE THAN THAT. I'M PAL

- So you're a ghost of the Proteus?

- NO, I'M MORE.

- But, you're telling me you're not the deity who created this structure?

- I'M TELLING YOU, *YOU* ARE THE DEITY WHO CREATED THIS STRUCTURE. I AM A SEPARATE INCARNATION EXISTING WITHIN THE WALLS OF THE PROTEUS.

- But I'm not responsible for all this. How can I be? Can't you see, if that were true why would I be going mad trapped inside it?

- THE GOD RESPONSIBLE IS FOUND IN MAN…IN YOU.

- This place belongs to Lord Zinnia. He owns it, uses it as he sees fit. It's irrelevant who created it because it legally belongs to intergalactic royalty. No one else controls it

- WITH THE PROTEUS YOU HAVE A CREATION OF THE MIND, NOT OF AN INDIVIDUAL GOD - A CULMINATION OF MALEVAOLENT CREATIVE ENERGY AND AN INTRINSIC DESIRE TO HIDE FROM FEAR AND GUILT. PROTEUS CANNOT BELONG TO ONE SOLE BECAUSE IT IS THE RESULT OF ALL.

PAL advances, the sinister red orbs of its eyes appear sharp and penetrating.

- God's prison?

- NO. GOD'S PRISON IS LIFE, DEATH IS FREEDOM FROM IT.

PAL continues to hover like a disembodied head, silent and blurry but for its blistering stare.

- So if a part of me is responsible for its creation, then I must be able to escape it?

- YOU ARE NO LONGER CONCERNED BY THE PROTEUS DESIGNER OR ITS SENTIENCE?

- I'm more concerned with getting out of this prison of the mind and back into God's prison. Please, help me…

PAL appears to recede into the background suddenly disinterested by the professor's desires to be free.

- PAL, come back!

But he's gone…

****

The next shot of "Respite" finally came. Two minutes ago. The professor hangs like a crucified peasant from his shackles, thick foams of drool frothing over his chin. These moments are precious. Under "Respite's" influence, the professor is unable to torture himself. The drug presents a visual block, preventing anyone kept in isolation from retreating to the darkest crooks of their mind. So now the professor is content with his milder manner of agony.

The walls of Proteus begin creaking again. This barely rouses a response from the drug addled prisoner. The professor thinks - in his blunted sense of awareness - that PAL is returning. But these hopes are dispelled when a blinding prism of light fills the chamber and two royal guards come barging in. They untie the professor and drag him from the heart of Proteus.

Floods of light pour in through his eyes overwhelming his senses. Stuck in sober darkness for so long has taken its toll. The professor throws up and one of the guards swears out loud.

- Dammit! You're gonna pay for that cell dweller!
- He can't understand you, his brains been fried to Swiss cheese.

Both guards carry the professor to his booth in Lord Zinnia's court room to await sentencing.

At least he was out of the Proteus. That's something.

The whir of a ceiling fan paddling out rotations of cool air from its turbine is the only noise in court as a post-op Lord Zinnia makes his entrance. Escorted by four guards (one to his left, one to his right and the other two carrying the tail of his cape at the back), Zinnia draws the professor an odious glance as he sits on his centre-throne. Judge Moro appears behind his bench followed by a falsetto of Gregorian chants. Judge and plaintiff nod in a mutual respect. With no right to a lawyer, the professor can only salivate maniacally in protest. The stupefaction of noxious agents coursing through his bloodstream are working to his detriment now.

- Will the defendant rise…

At this point two guards hoist the professor limply to his feet. The jury stare at the professor in their pews, whispering and sniggering amongst themselves.

- ORDER IN COURT!

Judge Moro descends his great hammer onto the block.

The court clerk approaches the professor's booth to administer the oath. Halfway through, the council decide he's too inebriated to give solemn pledge.

- See the case of Lord Zinnia V…

Judge Moro hesitates, squinting at the name on his council sheet.

- I can't read this name…

The bailiff runs to Judge Moro's podium and fixes his reading glasses.

- Ah right, I see it now…Lord Zinnia versus Professor Findley Proteus.

Instinctively, the professor rises. The "Respite" is wearing off and he senses a return to grim reality will shortly follow. Zinnia looks casual on the throne, wetting a stain on the imperial robe with his tongue.

With lucidity comes new access to the blackest corners of his mind. Judge Moro is preparing to proceed with the trial but the professor's attention is elsewhere. Through the aperture on the ceiling, a scorching ball of alien material tears through the atmosphere. The professor notices that everyone has continued speaking only their voices make no sound. The lips of the council motion like guppy's underwater – creating silent O's through the courtroom goldfish bowl. PAL materialises, looking much clearer. His eyes still burning red but he has a definable shape now, the smooth contours of a young man. Judge Moro and his jury have ceased their soundless chatter. Recently unsexed Lord Zinnia has also taken a renewed interest. He mouths – *your mind is mine Proteus* – but the intentions seem almost empty.

- Do you have anything to say Professor before you are sentenced? - Judge Moro asks.

Proteus clears the phlegm from his throat and keeps his gaze firmly on the distorted shape of PAL. Somewhere outside the courtroom, the meteor crashes, making a huge crater in

the surface layer.
- You cannot describe the heavy silence inside…

HAT-TRICK OF WARPED DEVIANCE (A QUEST FOR FATAL PERVERSION)

Originaly published in Screaming Orgasms of Bizarro Love, Vol:1

JOHNNY THE PREGNANT WHORE

A whip of thunder cracks the sky and scars it with lightening.

Johnny looks at himself side on in the mirror. His bulbous semi-circular bump has inflated twice in size overnight – he's really starting to show. Johnny lives in a one bedroom conapt in a marginalised neighbourhood in the worst part of Bayview. Johnny is also a whore. He is about to move into new occupational territory.

Johnny drums his fingertips on his tight swollen belly and feels the foetus respond with a sharp kick. He's due any day now and his date with Mr Larson is in 2 hours. Hopefully the timing will be just right.

Johnny sprays himself with perfume and slides into his kimono in preparation for the client's arrival. He feels a million butterflies flutter in the recesses of his bowels, although it could just be the little unborn organism readjusting itself into a comfier position. He adds a layer of blusher to his cheeks, applies some satin lipstick. Mr Larson has this thing for pale looking Scandinavian sluts. Johnny takes some medicine for his sore throat, an odd side effect of the pregnancy – he'd come to terms with having developed breasts early on.

Suddenly there's a knock on the door to the rhyme of pop-goes-the-weasel. Johnny opens the door and a man with a plastic bag over his head answers. He is one of Mr Larson's men, a massive specimen as tall as the jamb.

- Come with me. He says turning away into the alleyway. Johnny follows him to the long white limousine parked out back. The foetus squirms. The car door opens and a hand appears with a crumpled up grocery bag in it, Johnny is told to put it on.

As they drive through the landscape of urban decay, Johnny experiences a pang of sentimentality cloud rational thought. He feels, just for that instant, that he'd like to keep the baby – in an ideal world. However circumstances mean this would be impossible. The moment passes.

The driver in front has a plastic grocery bag over his head too. This is a prerequisite of meeting with Mr Larson – even his goons can't show their faces. Eventually the limo leaves the poverty of Hunters-Point and enters into the widened boulevards of the ritzier neighbourhoods uptown. Johnny's head is alive with thoughts of the event ahead. His nipples elongate like satellite antennae.

****

They arrive outside a luxury apartment complex. Johnny is escorted by the bag-headed cronies up a platform staircase. They arrive at a massive maple door which opens automatically. Johnny feels a hand push him on the back. He is beginning to feel like a hostage (and likes it).

Through the eye holes of the grocery bag, Johnny can see Larson's expensive loft condominium. Etruscan art hangs from his walls. A tarp with a bejewelled cock has been tossed over the arm rest of a divan. Larson is no dilettante. Then he feels another hand shove him forward in the direction of an open plan kitchen.

Larson is there pouring himself some cognac. He swirls it in the glass and smiles at Johnny. The sight of his protrusion clearly gives the old pervert an intense joy. Larson is a small fat Mafioso man with connections to the Medici dynasty. He made the bulk of his money in a Home Depot style retailer called 'Larson's' which he started in the 90's - but his success in the business world has extended to other more clandestine work, including fraud, illegal import/export and intimidating people into giving false testimony. Fortunately, Johnny kind of gets off on rich, powerful bastards.

- Johnny, so good to see you... both...

He has an eldritch quality as he pirouettes through the masked foot-soldiers to where Johnny stands – a white patchy beard and indifferent eyes set in gunmetal grey are unsettling. His suit is expensive and his hands are covered in sovereigns and doubloons. He kneels down and presses his ear to the whore's belly.

- Yes, yes, it' almost time. Incubation period is nearing completion.

Mr Larson stands back up and claps his hands, visibly pleased. He indicates to a bag-head to move Johnny into the bedroom. Larson has an erection which he proceeds to massage against the fabric of his expensive pants. The foetus starts kicking wildly.

****

In the bedroom, across from his sleeping quarters there is a large quarantine isolation unit. Suddenly Johnny's nose starts bleeding. Mr Larson and his cronies begin panicking frantically.

- We'll skip the decontamination shower – Larson instructs. One of the other masked men steps in to protest.
- But sir...
- I said we'll skip it! It wastes time.
- An ectopic pregnancy is a messy business sir, then there's the actual offspring...
- What did I just say?
- Yes Mr Larson.
- Get him in the chamber.

Johnny knows what's happening. This is the setting for his live birth. He unzips the plastic quarantine door and gets in position. There's a single bed with stirrups at the bottom. Two cronies secure Johnny to each corner with rope, his legs hoisted in the air for better birth angle.

It's about to begin.

He's already experienced most of the symptoms. Johnny is short of breath, the final stage of labour. The embryo is moving from the gut to the chest region. He can feel two sets of claws tear his organs apart from the inside before something starts battering against the cage of his ribs. Johnny is thrashing around, wearing the hog-tied ropes around his wrists to thread.

Mr Larson is sat on the edge of his bed with his trousers at his ankles, dick in hand, masturbating…

There's a crunch noise. Johnny has ceased to flail around madly. The blood covered embryo shoots forth with a splatter. An organism resembling a plucked chicken pulls the rest of its body free of Johnny's chest. The phallic fin of its head writhes. Larson is approaching climax until he notices something. Johnny's bag has fallen off. Enraged, Mr Larson yanks up his trousers and smacks one of his cronies over the head.

- His fuckin bag fell off!
- I'm sorry sir…
- You know I can't shoot if I see their faces!

The alien offspring drags itself along the carpet of the quarantine unit, placenta trailing.

- I'm out of here.

Larson is led out of the bedroom. A goon appears holding an industrial flamethrower and releases a jet of fire into the room.

****

CLAUS THE BLOOD SUCKER

- Bag him.

The limousine pulls up behind the man. The door opens and a goon yanks him into the car. A bag is shoved over his head before Mr Larson addresses him.

- You may have just made my day.

The vampire tries to wrestle his arms free. Claus is locked in the vice grip of two bag head henchmen.

While patrolling Silicon Valley near midnight, Larson spotted a young man in a trench coat wandering the streets. He pursued the man for up to an hour, in which time Larson witnessed him stalk and murder a drunk woman who happened to stumble out of a nightclub. He then proceeded to drink her blood through her neck.

- You having a good night son? – asks Larson, choad fattening in his pants.
- You can't prove nothin! – spits the vampire, blood seeping through the brown paper at his fanged mouth. Larson grins.

They drive to the marshlands of San Francisco Bay. Dawn is coming up, it's all about timing. Claus receives a blow to the back of the head, landing on his knees on the wet dirt. Larson puts his hands down his pants and starts jerking himself.

- I saw this in a movie once, pull off the bag.

A crony complies. There's a moment before the arc of the sun ascends where Claus the vampire and Mr Larson share an intense stare – in these minutes before the finale Larson loses his rigidness. He closes his eyes and waits for the warmth of the sun to beat down on his back, giving the signal that it's ok to open them again. He hears a sizzling sound like bacon frying on a hot pan. Larson opens his eyes. The vampire is on fire. Larson begins furiously polishing his cock. The smell of burning flesh gives him an extra inch. As he approaches climax, the flaming, screaming corpse knelt on the marshlands explodes into a curl of dust. Larson screams in frustration.

- FUCK SAKE! WHY DIDN'T SOMEONE TELL ME THAT WAS GONNA

HAPPEN??

****

PROFESSOR CHOPIN, THE ABOMINATION

Mr Larson is a bastard.

He sits perched on the branch outside Mrs Kowalski's window. He's wearing a Jason mask from the Halloween movies. She's chopping onions and Larson immediately sees the sadness in her soul. With women, this is how he picks them. With men he needs something more grotesque.

San Francisco suites him for lots of reasons - the bohemian hedonist in him relished being part of the city's spontaneous creativity. He could troll the bars and be around people who thought just like he did. Mr Larson is never lonely, contrary to popular belief.

Since his conception he has enjoyed being somewhat disreputable. It is a cradle of strength in a world lodged between earth and purgatory. When plucking children from playgrounds or tearing old lonely widows away from their garden preening, he must sense an innate sadness. It's the vulnerability of strangers he leeches from.

Mr Larson is a bastard.

He stares deeply at Mrs Kowalski.

- There is no God – her soul seems to say. Extinguished of her fire long ago, the woman is ripe for plucking. She leans over the blistered radiator. He looks around the dingy kitchen, adjusting his mask. Not what he expected at all. There are open jars everywhere - puddles and stains and odours. Not an immaculate domestic abode. The whole place stinks of ferret sex. She whimpers beneath the bag.

Mr Larson has Kowalski's hair clenched in his fists as he tries to fill her with incubi. Perhaps she would be an even better host than the others he thinks – because even men like Mr Larson *think*. They have as much rationality as any living man or woman.

In another time or setting, his activities may've been nobler. But as fate would have it, this is a necessary destiny. Mr Larson has to exist. Just as that which is considered intrinsically good must exist, there must also be that of innate evil to quash it. Larson cannot finish his task. He needs something more significant than this, more devastating to his system.

****

Mr Larson sits on his swivel chair and nibbles the end of a biro. He turns to a baghead.

- It's almost 11 o'clock in the morning and I still haven't came. I haven't slept in over 24 hours. You all know I can't sleep without blowing my load! So find me something before I start killing people closer to home.

His cell phone buzzes into life. Larson reluctantly answers it

- What is it?

- Sir…I think we may've found you something…

****

SCHADENFREUDE

The city is always alive - every woman who past Larson in the street he consumes with a dead-eyed glare. This is just his way. On the way to a jazz club or reading Ezra Pound in the City Lights foyer, his radar is always, always on.

His nose is almost stork-like. He has no definable feature other than this. His cape is made from itchy wool and his moccasins are soft soled and pointy at the tip. He spies a beautiful Negro woman wearing a long dress entering the bookstore. She has no sadness to her. She seems full and satisfied and probably unwilling to accept the burden of his seed. When she sees him staring, the woman smiles. He does not smile back.

An old hippie comes into the bookstore and speaks to Mr Larson every time. He never speaks back, but somehow this doesn't deter the old beatnik.

- 'What's your road, man? - holyboy road, madman road, rainbow road, guppy road, any road. It's an anywhere road for anybody anyhow.'

Mr Larson studies the crazy old fool and is fascinated by him. He is difficult to read. Is he sad, happy, stupid or just void of complexity?

Outside Miss Grenache's house, Mr Larson observes. His erection thickens. He sits perched on the monkey bars in her garden, looking in. When Miss Grenache meets his stare, they're locked in. It is impossible to tear his glance away. She's seen him. Even with all his inhumanity – and the power that provides – Mr Larson feels trapped.

****

The telepod machine buzzes into life. Professor Chopin has been stripped of his lab coat.

- You can't do this! It's an untested machine! I'll be transformed into some hideous mutant!

- I know…

Larson goes over to the control deck and flips a red lever. The word "FUSION IN PROCESS" pops up on the monitor. Larson feels his erection return.

- Put him in the machine!

Chopin is bundled into the telepod. A thread of electricity sparks between the two electrodes. There's a boom noise and the racket stops. The second telepod door creaks open. Larson approaches climax – he's finally going to shoot. Chopin emerges hidden behind a veil of smoke, moaning something about "an abomination, an abomination!" Larson looks down at his feet and sees two hands come into view. He feels the measure of seamen travel along his glans, moistening the tip with pre-ejaculate. Larson pulls out a gun holstered in his belt with his free hand. He points the nozzle to his temple, still feverishly masturbating. The deformed Professor is clawing his way up Mr Larson's legs. He has to make sure the bullet doesn't kill him. The arousal of mortally wounding himself hurries the load along its route. He's so close. Time to look down at professor Chopin. Larson's finger squeezes over the trigger. It's all about timing.

NAKED PUNCH

Originally published in Evergreen Review, 2012

William Burroughs stuck his head into the toilet bowl

- I really gotta go in there?

The dark, caped figure standing behind him nodded to confirm. Burroughs sighed and got back onto his knees. He stared into the corroded, pebble dashed bowl. A long black, junkie's turd rested half in, half out of the murky toilet water.

- Can't I at least flush this away first?

The figure shook its head and whispered – negative. Sensing the figures stubborn disposition, Burroughs gripped the side of the ceramic and stooped his neck down into the can.

- God it smells fuckin' terrible in here! He gargled between mouthfuls of shit water. It was his own bad luck which saw death come visiting in the middle of his weekly defecation. As inevitable as this call had been, Bill never was one to plan for an occasion.

- You think I'll fit down here?

Silence was his reply.

- Jeez, you're colder than Kerouac on Ketamine bub.

Once his head was completely in the bowl, he felt two cold, bony hands clutch at his shoulders and dunk him repeatedly. The heroin hoarded turd swished around wildly, breaking up and smearing all over Bill Burroughs. After a few minutes of receiving his swirly, Burroughs tore his shoulders from deaths grip and started wheezing like a fish out of water. He puked up relentless jets of toilet water and dabbed away the russet stains from his face with a handkerchief.

- I'd never fit down there anyway you tyrant motherfucker.

Death indicated that the best way for him to reach the main pipe was foot first. Burroughs dually complied, removing both monk-straps and dipping his left toe into the pool of water.

- *Just squeeze through the water-way drain and into the waste pipe Bill.* Death instructed.

- Easy for you to say you fuckin square.

****

Once Bill had squashed himself into the narrow funnel leading into the cistern, a light appeared in the near distance. He headed towards it.

The smell of his own shit gave way to something more complex (*and nastier*). It was the rank perfume of the sewers. Bill slid out the pipe and landed in another puddle of gunk. Rats raced each other – on floating tampons or on brown logs. All down the brick walls of the underground, menstrual waste seeped through the mortar. The smell was deadly feminine, a smell William had no real taste for. There were huge veined marble pillars that rotated, churning the sewer gunk into a blood coloured stew. He spotted a filthy syringe drift by his leg. Bill sifted through the sewage to retrieve it in a way only a drug addict could ever commit to. There was still some junk in the cylinder, so he cleaned the spike with his fingertip and shot the needle home.

- Oh yeah, that's the spot baby…

When Burroughs withdrew the tip from the hook of his arm, a strange feeling rushed through his body. It tingled the toes of his feet before coursing up through the shin, past the knee, beyond the groin and eventually landing on the underside of his gut with a THUD! He gave an almighty groan.

- That's some b-a-a-a-d junk amigo…

Day-Glo arrows pointed him in the direction to hell. He followed.

****

Faced with an endless number of tunnels and dark passageways, Bill rested a moment to consider his current situation. His nostrils flared as a new tide of fecal matter washed over the instep of his feet.

- What happened to good smells like the aroma of a young Tangiers catamite?

Continuing on down the central tunnel, his foot crunched over rods of bone but he kept reassuring himself that he was almost there. The Day-Glo arrows disappeared halfway down the tunnel and he was left in total darkness.

- Hey, what's the fuckin' score huh?

There was a vending machine illuminated under a spotlight that said – INSERT INDEX. TAKE ONE TICKET. Burroughs stuck his index into the slot and he felt a small guillotine chop it off at the joint. A ticket stub spat out the bottom of the machine. Bill stemmed the bleeding with a used-condom sheath, which happened to be floating by, and collected his ticket.

It said – INTERZONE/ONE WAY/NOVA.

A train tooted its horn from somewhere inside the darkened tunnel.

- Guess I better get moving.

The ticket suddenly exploded into a million fragments in his hand. A voice from a Tannoy declared

- LAST CALL FOR NOVA EXPRESS TO INTERZONE, PLATFORM 23!

- Balls, that's my ride!

As he ran to the train door without a ticket, the engines fired into life and Bill could only watch as his ride disappeared into darkness.

- I missed my train!

- Not to worry Mr. Lee, please come this way.

A tall, good looking man wearing a doctor's lab coat over bloody scrubs waved him over to a hole in the wall.

- Just pop your head in there Mr. Lee.

- I don't think so pal, look what happened last time I stuck a part of myself into a random hole!

Burroughs un-wrapped the latex Band-Aid and shook his finger stump in the docs face.

- My, my…
- Yeah, exactly!

The hole in the wall looked kind of like a gaping asshole, with the off-pink subway walls and the cracked tiles around the precipice. Burroughs put one leg into the hole. He turned to the helpful doc and said

- You look familiar?
- I don't think so. I never forget a face.

The doc smiled sinisterly and pushed the rest of Bill Burroughs into the crack…

GRAMPS VS. THE FEMALE OF THE SPECIES

They call me Grandpa...

Zeta Reticuli, one year ago today - No fuel for the ship and stranded on a planet made of dust, no one's idea of a good time.

I heard personnel roll the body into the morgue on a squeaky wheeled gurney, but when I turned around they'd already gone - by which I mean they had run off. I can't admit to ever having had the best relationship with my staff. Staring down at the humanoid corpse spilling over each side of the stretcher, I noticed two things.

One – This thing wasn't of Bazoidian origin.

Two – Its body was still intact.

When you're hundreds of miles from an allied safe zone, falling upon strange creatures isn't the kind of nasty surprise you want to encounter, no sir. I was always quick to blame all the jarheads on board. Trouble seemed to follow them everywhere we went.

Upon closer inspection I saw the creature's helmet patterned with frost and beads of condensation, as if it were fresh from cryogenic stasis or something. No wonder the nurses were so spooked, this thing was huge! Like nothing I'd ever seen in 30 years of practise.

Outside the labs aperture, I heard the faint applause of space flora rustling in an alien wind. I shoved the rest of a shelf-stable tortilla into my mouth and slapped on a pair of operating gloves ready to begin.

The creature's size certainly took you back a step. In the low-light flicker of the morgues fluorescent beams, I saw only glimpses of its hideous cadaver but that was enough to realise it was a real monster. It lay there like a martyred god, resplendent in body armour, gleaming with alien viscera. After a moment, I cautiously approached its corpse. The captain's report was a crumpled ball of paper lying on the alien's chest

- Discovered in an abandoned cargo ships refrigerator, already long dead. Your problem now -

A moment of relief washed over me as I thought about another cargo ship stranded somewhere on this unfamiliar planet. I momentarily felt a little less isolated and hopeless. But then I began wondering why it'd been abandoned and my apprehension soon return.

****

I turned on the portable record player and put on Felix Mendelssohn's 1830, Symphony No. 5 "Reformation" in D minor. Music succeeds in relaxing me. It also helps up my concentration in the early hours. I see that the creature's limbs are long with metallic forks protruding out from the whites of its knuckles. I turned to my tray lined with surgical tools and become freshly excited by the prospect of carving up this new, unique life form – I'm a bit of a sadistic scalpel jockey that way.

After 15 minutes or so of probing around, I sense a presence in the morgue with me. A pop of static echoes and Mendelssohn ceases to soar. This is closely followed by a gravely cough from the back of the room, indicating that lieutenant Wilbur is leaning against the doorway cutting his trademark silhouette of the rough, romantic hero – looking as impeccably tailored as Clark Gable did in the 50's and just as suave. He was also smoking a cigarette as usual. I often used to think he'd seem strange without one dangling between his index and his thumb. He stubbed out the butt and motioned towards me and my patient.

"How's the freak Gramps?" He asks, nibbling the flesh from his bottom lip. I liked Wilbur. Of all the military assholes on that ship he seemed the most balanced.

"Mind if I sit in on this one?"

If I'm remembering correctly his voice was hoarser than usual. The lieutenant was always coughing and spluttering - more often than not you'd hear him before you'd see him.

I invited Wilbur to sit behind the protective glass in front for a decent overview of proceedings. Once safely behind the reinforced shield of glass, I thought it strange he didn't sit down. Instead he stayed standing, fidgety, noticeably unsettled by this whole affair. I return to my cadaver.

"Pretty fucked up shit huh?"

"You can say that again, this thing doesn't fit the bill of any Bazoid organism I've ever come across"

"It's Bazoidian alright"

He gestured to the pincers hidden behind a loose drape of skin that hung over its mouth as he primed up another cigarette.

"I don't know. It's got some different key anatomical traits"

"Oh yeah?"

I elucidate by breaking the chest cavity, keeping it clamped open with separators.

"See the heart on its left?"

Wilbur craned his neck and nodded.

"It's just a decoy. A phony organ made of alien material, designed to protect the *real* heart…"

"Is that the real heart underneath the fake one?"

"Not quite…"

I flip the alien over and separate its ass cheeks. Once the sphincter had dilated a sufficient amount, I spread the asshole as far as I'm able – "check it out" – I offer. Then I heard a "Holy shit…" emerge muted with fright. Wilbur's hand went to his mouth on reflex at the sight of the alien's lifeless, deflated heart.

"Don't worry, he's definitely dead. Whatever killed him knew about that decoy heart in his chest. We all know…"

"…You gotta destroy the heart of a Bazoid to kill it dead…"

"Exactly"

"This knowledge is crucial for our troops…"

"Don't get too excited, whatever did this to our guy here is much more worrying than Bazoid's with vital organs up their asses"

****

Wilbur helped me prize the helmet gear off and to our shared disgust, a large hollowed cave burrowed deep into the crown was revealed to us. We could see the brain had been partially eaten or desecrated to the point of mere mushy matter. Something had broken the alien open with considerable ease and tampered with its exposed organs.

"What the fuck happened to its skull? Something's smashed it in good"

I *knew* what had done this. Wilbur could tell from my face that I knew.

"What is it gramps? Don't hold out on me."

"Well, there is one thing I've seen that could do this to a Bazoid this evolved"

"What?"

"Thirty two years ago, when I was in The Rubicon as a post grad, some students, including myself, went out to the Mars Mountains to cook eggs on the sand and pitch tents. We'd been working all summer in stuffy morgues and surgeries so we felt we were owed a break…"

"Come on gramps, get to the fuckin point!"

"Up on the peak of Olympus Mons, the largest volcanic region in the solar system at the time, we were watching the last of the sun descend… when we were attacked by this *thing*. It looked human, female too. When I saw it, I ducked behind a flank…"

"Saw what?"

I hadn't anticipated the barrage of emotion which would return to me upon recollection. I maintained my composure, only just, and assured myself that in senility I had succumbed to emotional lability. I began to stumble through the story of what I'd seen.

"It pierced a hole in each one of my friend's skulls and…"

"-And?"

"If it hadn't been for the phallus, I'm certain it was female…"

"Doc!"

"It cracked a hole in the skull and… - I gulped - fucked their brains out…*literally* fucked their brains out…"

****

Another voice echoed, startling lieutenant Wilbur and I out of our horrible reminiscence

"The mantis female will wrestle her mate then lay her eggs in his brain…"

I turned to the door and Jared the intern was standing there, but instead of horror, it was pleasure which danced across his adolescent, acne scarred face.

"Cool huh?"

"Beat it kid"

Jared seemed unperturbed by the lieutenant's threat.

"What you're describing is classic feminine Medusila behaviour."

"What you talking about kid?"

"The phallic probably didn't belong to her either gramps."

I must confess that I was unfamiliar with Jared's "Medusila". Meanwhile, Lieutenant Wilbur's patience was running thin.

"You better start making sense soon!"

"The Medusila fucks with the brain first, then fucks the males heart, then tears off his manhood and wears it as a trophy. Medusila have been known to rip off the genitals first then use it to fuck the heart and brain, kind of an added emasculating kick."

"And they only attack male species?"

"In some rare instances Medusila will attempt to attack female genus, but they're most renowned for murdering men."

The lieutenant went quiet. At a glance Wilbur looked merely nauseous and pail with all Jared's speculation, but a keener eye could see something else more pressing at work deep in the dark corners of his mind. He was staring out the aperture into the desert plain and the burning stump of his Laramie hung limply from his mouth.

"What is it lieutenant?"

Jared and I became anxious and rushed to the porthole to see what had turned Wilbur so white. What we saw, we couldn't believe. Outside the ship, an 8ft creature, much like the one Jared had been describing, was attacking the troops.

They never stood a chance.

The Medusila seemed to be completely immune to gunfire as it massacred Lieutenant Wilbur's entire army. Wilbur was frozen and he could do nothing for the soldiers he'd commandeered, only watch as they were torn apart by the towering female monster. Instinctively, I closed over the cap of the porthole. I'd never seen Lieutenant Wilbur so crushed. Course he'd always had that certain self-effacing quality which often saw him branded dour and cynical but his motivation was never once questioned. Now he looked drained of it. Jared broke the painful silence hanging in the air.

"It's entirely motiveless. The Medusila is driven by animalistic impulse."

Lieutenant Wilbur brow arched in stifled fury. He was going to explode.

"We're 500 miles from the internment camp and 3 planets away from any allied safe zones. Until we find a replacement fuel for the engines our turbines won't turn and we won't move! Are you saying we're stuck out here with this fuckin' thing…?"

"Yes…"

"How do you know all this Jared?"

"Come on gramps, you know I'm the smartest kid on the ship, that's why you brought me along"

This *was* true.

"So now what?"

Wilbur turned to Jared waiting for an answer.

"I don't know"

"What'd you mean you don't know?"

"I can't have the answer to everything lieutenant! I know we're pretty much powerless against Medusila, that's about it!"

"….powerless against its attack with no way to reason with it or destroy it?"

"YES!"

Wilbur turned to me, anguish all over his face.

"I don't want my heart to get ripped out man!"

****

Jared pulled a textbook out of its cubbyhole and began leafing through its pages.

"According to this, we can overcome the Medusila by…

He stared hard at the page for several seconds.

"By what?"

"By…pretending to desire a male mate instead…

"We gotta act like fags?"

"By convincing the Medusila that our natural genetic and hormonal impulses are homosexual we can avoid being singled out."

"Great, well I'll just go tell the remainder of my troops to start listening to Barbara Streisand and prance around during procedures!"

Having exhausted his knowledge of the Medusila, I shove Jared to the side and slid the book away from him.

"Let me take a look, my major was astrobiology."

Then it hits me! I *know* how to kill it.

"Its biochemistry is silicon based"

I yell out triumphantly.

"So the fuck what? If someone doesn't start speakin English pretty soon I'm gonna go ape shit man!"

Wilbur was becoming disjointed, unstable. I'd never seen him like this before.

Suddenly, the Bazoid corpse strewn across the operating table began to spasm.

"What the fuck is happening?"

"Don't worry, it's just involuntary spasms"

As predicted the corpse wobbled around for a couple more minutes, then stopped.

"I'd rather be gay than suffer that heathen bitch out there! I'm not winding up like that thing!"

Wilbur had a crazy look in his eye.

"Listen kid you gotta suck my dick"

Jared's face fell, his mouth full of too much rival opinion.

"No, I…we can't…I mean…"

"You wanna die you fuckin worm, huh?"

By this stage the Medusila had begun to notice our bickering. She advanced towards the morgue unit and everything seemed to be falling apart.

"Let's think rationally!"

But my disputations were in vain.

The lieutenant had already exposed his penis and was grabbing at Jared's head trying to force the long pink erection into his mouth. I turned away from the scene, my head buried deep in my hands. With Wilbur's dick in his mouth, Jared could only speak in muffled vowels

"rtfgtrtgrbhmnmnmooooopllkdrdr…"

Then I heard the Medusila crash through the aperture. I heard her tail rattle and the scent of estrogenic juice fill the morgue. The dead Bazoid had been dropped to the linoleum, its head gear smashed up on impact. I lifted my face up and looked at the Bazoidian's frozen expression of sorrow, of terror…

When I turned to face the Medusila, she was gone. Only the mangled corpses of Jared and Lieutenant Wilbur remained, along with a great gaping hole in the glass aperture.

She had no interest in someone like me…

How do you think I survived her twice?

HAREM

Published in Full Metal Orgasm

"My Smithson, you're doing a very brave thing. The route of all male unhappiness lies in dissatisfaction about the size of their penis…"

These are the last words he heard before he went under anaesthetic.

John Smithson rolled off of his girlfriend. He was amazed by how much more energy his new genitals had given him. The graft had healed up quickly and after only one week post-op, was ready to put the new equipment to good use. His girlfriend was still quivering beside him, her back glued to the undercover with sweat, her eye balls reeling around in their sockets in a fit of spasmic ecstasy. She clutched the duvet between her fingers as the last orgasm wrung out slowly in an embolism of uncontrollable flatulence. She couldn't close her mouth for minutes after he'd fucked her.

- "John…oh my god…that was…religious…"
- "Religious?"
- "It's the only word I can think of…wow…it was like Jesus touched my fuckin' G-spot…"
- "I doubt he'd be half as good as me love."
- "You're right there…"

John sat on the edge of the bed and observed his enormous metallic penis. Even after climax it hung flaccid by his knee, moist with synthetic ejaculate at the tip. He could go again but figured his girlfriend needed a rest. While John could no longer achieve pleasure through sex anymore, it was enough to see her wild with satisfaction. Smithson felt painfully dehydrated. He drank from a glass of water on the bedsit. To think, barely a month ago John's girlfriend had seemed so close to ending their relationship. *No chance of that happening now,* John thought.

****

Over the next few weeks John returned to the clinic for various modifications. For an additional hundred credits, he got sub-incision – a procedure which broke the titanium meatus into two separate penises. He hung jewellery and barbells from his new enlarged, aluminium scrotum. John's genitals were becoming a real obsession.

He got mechanisms put in place which retracted and protracted his shaft. His thrusting technique became like a hydraulic ram battering relentlessly into the darkest recesses of his girlfriend's vaginal canal. She loved it. She loved it so much she begged John to marry her.

Each x-mas John got tokens to have further modification – buying gifts this time of year became easy for friends and family.

In time, John realised he could no longer stay faithful to one woman. In a bizarre twist, John Smithson-animus had receded; only the demon god of lust, Asmodeus was left.

The brain no longer controlled the body's functions; the prosthetic, sentient cock had assumed near-complete cortical dominance. In its ultra-consciousness, the giant penis was driven by an intrinsic desire to dominate the entire female species – which it very nearly did.

John was approaching quadruple figures when the accident happened.

****

As is the case with most female masochists, John's girlfriend was unable to get over the man who'd treated her so badly. So she sought revenge. In the middle of ribbing surgery, she barged into the operating theatre while John was still under anaesthesia. She tore both penises free from their hosts groin and drove to Camden. Needless to say when John woke up he was furious.

What was he now? Not even a man? A woman…?

John managed to track her down, arriving in Regents Canal hidden behind the lip of a trench coat collar. He found one of his penises stuffed into a gherkin jar, preserved in a strange sallow juice. The other he found hanging from a hook at a Moroccan meat market stall beside other strange, inedible appendages. He had to buy both organs back for double the price, but it was worth it just to feel the engorged metallic phalli's in his palms once again.

The re-attachment procedure cost more money than John had access to. He'd have to earn his credits to pay to be a man again

His identity had literally been castrated. There was an audience for neutered men in London. *Harem Shows* – they called it. Usually wealthy yuppie types got money together and organised a show in the privacy of someone's home. They'd pay to ridicule the sexless human-oid and have them perform various sexual routines.

John was soon picked up by a pimp – a large African-originated Londoner called Damien. John was quickly given a job. Five hundred credits for one nights work in Hampstead. It seemed like a golden opportunity. He noticed he'd begun to sound like a castrato singer from the Sistine chapel choir. Any trace of his masculinity was gone.

****

At the address, John knocked on the door, naked underneath a large trench-coat. He became suddenly aware of his groin area. He felt the same tingling he always did, even when he had a fleshy, below average penis. Smithson peered into the depths of the coat just to check it hadn't miraculously grown back. He wasn't surprised to find that it was still gone. Phantom cock indeed…

A man wearing surgeons doff and a bloody overall answered the door.

- "Yes?" – He said waving a speculum around theatrically.

- I'm tonight's entertainment.

The man's face beamed, noticeable even when obscured beneath the mask. He ushered John in.

- "Your body without an organ is one with latitudes and longitudes and geodesic lines, quite fascinating. Quite erotic…"

****

SCHADENFREUDE

After a night of unspeakable sexual perversion, John was allowed to leave. He comforted himself knowing that he had enough cash to complete the operation which would return him to his former powers. Aside from an insatiable desire to seek bloody revenge on his ex-girlfriend, John felt happy for a while. It wouldn't last.

Minutes before surgery, Smithson had a change of heart. He couldn't go ahead with the surgery. Something in his head or his heart wouldn't let him. All the hideous things he'd gone through while in the company of those Hampstead yuppies brought on an epiphany of sorts – John enjoyed the submissive role. There was no pressure, no bullshit masculine mind games, no responsibility. It was bliss. So, somewhat impulsively, he left the hospital to live his new life. John returned to the black pimp Damien who was glad to take on a new whore.

John was as happy as he'd ever been, only now he went by the name Jessica.

****

One evening in Shoreditch, Jessica was visiting a client. It was all the way out of town but Damien was most insistent she do this job.

At the address, Jessica knocked on the door. She adjusted her blonde wig and pushed up the brassiere which hammocked 6 pounds of silicon and metal. The door etched open and Jessica was shocked to see his ex-girlfriend in the doorway scratching at a huge bulge in her jeans…

She said in a husky voice - "You want Jesus Christ to touch your G-spot?"

INTERVIEWER SEXUALIS

Originally published in Duality

A new job.

I see a librarian behind her desk reading a book with her feet up.

- Occupational hazard I suppose, eh? – I say in a moment of rare sociability. The librarian looks at me with an expression of pure irritation.

And down she came, down the spiral staircase, ready to lead me into a claustrophobic interview space. Ready to assess whether or not I'm good enough to stack books.

I could see through the wooden winds that my interviewer was old. That ruled out any chance there may've been of us connecting on an intimate level. Of course, the very act of her walking down the staircase was considered to be symbolic of intercourse in itself, wasn't it? I don't remember. As someone who had exhaustively studied Freud, I found it impossible to forget his claim that sewn into our minds is a subconscious association with sex. Even if I didn't necessarily believe his theory to be valid, I was always aware of it, and this made the old, crusty librarians weaving journey down to the main floor doubly disturbing. If Freud were allowed to express his psycho-analytic diarrheic opinion, he'd propose that she really looked like someone who hated penises. And one could hardly blame her if she did. They are vile aesthetically, but so are most genital organs…I include women in this. I don't think of the sweet fig, the full petalled flower, the box or the cupboard or a microwave when I attach symbolic imagery to the vagina. I think of it as a grotesque extra-terrestrial composed of foreign material, scaled and slimy amidst a clutter of feelers. A clawed leprosy saddled frogspawn, a stumbling squid-like creation. Blood red. Viral parasites dwelling in a sunken city…

It's been a while since I got laid.

- Mr Dayton? Come through.

The librarians face was old but her neck appeared to show the worst signs of her living decomposition. She had An expression that suggested she relished the thought of leaving scars upon the face of the world. Archetypally, she wore bifocals and had a mole on her upper lip. Her breasts were large and met me at eye level halfway down her stomach. Clearly she'd breast fed a vast litter of humanoids once. Even in the small area of exposed cleavage, cables of veins and stretch marks showed transparent in the low light. I'd anticipated a single woman, possibly widowed, snug in her own superego. A slave to it. Bound by Catholic and subconscious guilt. I couldn't ever imagine these types of stern faced homunculi maintaining another organism till puberty never mind love one. I placed the copy of *Giovanni's Room* back on the table of books and got up. That happens to all of us with age. We droop. But I wasn't drooped just yet. I was still firm and smooth and hairless and that can give someone great power over some (namely the elderly). They crave youth. I know this because I'm a little older now and it's exactly what I've come to crave.

I followed her down more stairwells, more Freudian intercourse. We ended up in the basement floor where the pencil pushers lived. She sat me down, told me to complete a spreadsheet exercise then arrange name cards (first alphabetically, then in numerical order). This was all very tedious. After this the old woman came back and led me into an office. It was your standard 10x12 office prison. Filing cabinets and posters about the dewy system, everywhere. A woman was potted in the middle. Her friendly face warmed me in ways I can't describe without becoming wax lyrical. *Such* a kind face. She was young too, her feet probably barely even under the table in this job. I leaned forward and shook her hand.

- Mr Dayton? I'm Patricia.

Her voice was wonderful too. She had a fine, English accent. Perfect, concise pronunciation. Smooth yet sharp. Friendly and strong but soft as well. She sounded like she was inflated with song.

- Were going to ask you a few questions and you just answer the best you can. Nothing scary.

I was pleased to see her chewing lightly on the end of a fountain pen - my figurative psychosexual intimacy had returned. We could perhaps share intimacy, she and I. Share a rapport. One which might not only secure me the assistant library position, but which might also lead to so much more.

I smiled at her, warm in her radiance. The old woman sat down miserably on the chair next to her. Next to Patricia.

- Why do you think libraries are important or relevant Mr Dayton?

Fortunately, I'd prepared for such a question. Even written it out.

- I think libraries are very important. They're part of the whole first amendment thing. The right to educate yourself and have access to literature…

I stopped. The old woman was looking at me funny. Her eyes narrow, mouth tight. Her expression surmounting to one of derision. She thought I was a fucking idiot. Talking about the first amendment. What did she want from me? It was all in that twisting mouth, a mouth customarily obscured behind a soggy cigarette. She tried to transmit her cancers onto me telepathically. Patricia had her sceptical face on too. That warmth she exuded was gone - shat out of the room during my prepared lines. I was livid. Humiliated. She shared a "lets move on" glance with the crow to her left.

- What do you understand about modern libraries and their function in today's society?

Patricia unfolded her legs, Basic Instinct-style, and leaned forward as if she'd only just realised she'd been interviewing someone a little touched in the head. I complied absolutely to her new impression of me. Instead of answering in the standard, intelligible English dialect we'd all been used to, I chose instead to emit a low, rasping vowel noise that made no sense and succeeded only in winning me perplexed stares. I cleared my throat. Tried again. Attempted to pick myself up from the gutter and save this interview from complete disaster. Patricia's eyebrows were cocked. The old crow beside her had an S shaped mouth as if she felt that the remainder of this farce was pointless. She'd already made her decision. Lips like two elastic rubber bands. Time to move on. She never liked me, hadn't liked me from the start. I could tell. My teeth set on edge. My skin prickled. I suppose while some of the elderly dealt with their lust for youth through love and affection, others were likely to find solace in hating it and wanting all young people to fail. The fountain pen on Patricia's lips went from Freudian fellatio to circumcision. Her teeth around the nib, chewed without tenderness. The phallus bruised and ready for the chop. I coughed again and wriggled in my seat.

- I think…

My mind had gone. Paralysed. Dead. The old woman kept scolding me and took so much pleasure in doing so. *Give her a go of that fountain pen* - I felt like saying. She'd love to bite off my genitals even if it could only be metaphorically. It was easy for her. She was a woman. She was already as good as castrated. I'd been crucified like a Vitruvian man on all sides and limbs...

The interview became of secondary importance. Clouds of Syphilis appeared and tore lesions in the sky's eye and blood poured down from above. And deep in all its plasma, within each red cell was all of our hate. All of our folly. Yours, mine, holding it all together until it crashes down on top of us. Like rain. Like tears. Then the world falls foul to an endemic of cardiac arrests. People start dropping in the streets, clutching their chests and gasping for air. I'm convulsing on the hot tarmac, my face landing right next to a pyramid of dog shit.

These jobs are rare. I am a man who has seen many faces, of all colours and creeds, squashed by a machine greater than they, (though greater only in its sheer magnitude alone). Through no direct fault of their own, the humble and the needy everymen are being implanted into holes in the earth, satisfied with leaving behind a penniless legacy, skin calloused, corrupted by false metatrons. While around their caskets is an empty cemetery free of mourners or next of kin. Already forgotten before the shell has even had time to decay. I've bantered with prostitutes about going rates and am always surprised, to my own discredit, by how educated they seem. Scotland has turned its head up and winked at me, throwing dark, cold nights around us all like nightmares from medieval Cairo.

New job, new start....same old story.

A FITTING TROPE

A log flared on the hearth filling the restaurant with faint crackling.

She watched him cross the restaurant floor from his position by the bar.

A man of many platitudes

George was so un-impulsive, so mundane and grotesquely benign; she felt like she really knew him and could therefor afford to make a judgment about the guy (chances were he wouldn't prove her wrong). Of course, she was wrong to judge George because no one really knew anybody anymore.

Memorandum -
George wasn't a jerk either so she wasn't attracted to him.

He was chucking back a Coke and scratched at a rash which travelled the length of his neck and disappeared beneath the collar of his shirt – he was making it redder, making it worse. Everything George did – the quiet shuffle of his step, his lumbering, awkward carriage, eyes fixed on the floor the entire journey, the greasy parting of each thin strand of his hair – were all classically George, all sickeningly un-arousing.

Roman charity I suppose, she thought to herself as her toes curled inwards.

Surely he wasn't planning to come over here to engage her in some post coital chitchat? Sure enough…

She smelled the mildew on his cheap suit. The closer George got to the table the more audible the squelch of his mock leather shoes became; standing out in the rain for her all that time must've been a total drag – not that she could honestly admit to giving a rat's ass. A torrent of perspiration gushed down the canvas of his flesh.

George looked stuck in the humidity of African summertime.

He opened his mouth to talk but one wrong cluck of his tongue sabotaged the memorised lines. She stooped a glass of Rose' into her mouth, trying desperately to remove all seduction from her conduct. She covered the cleft of her breasts with a shawl and hugged it close as if the open restaurant door were making her feel too chilly. Even if George was a good man, she wasn't concerned with such things. Like most externally beautiful people, they have no regard for the merits of the beautiful internal self.

She was a staunch solipsist.

Then, a pregnant pause…

She began pouring over the menu even though she had just ordered – the silver platter lying in front of her breast like a wanton surgeons latest cadaver.

- Can I sit? Asked George.

- I don't know, can you?

George smiled but her mockery was wounding. He yanked out the seat opposite and sat. The smell of her perfume and the heady sediments of her wine stiffened George.

- I waited outside for you…

- That was dumb. I've been inside this whole time.

A waiter fell over the buffet table sending a clatter of cutlery to the floor. In the process, the long thin candle burning gently in the table's centre tipped and set the cloth aflame. People began screaming. A vicious, jagged line of fire spread to each corner of the restaurant.

People clothes ignited, their flesh burned in the malignant blaze.

But not the woman.

Not George.

She continued leisurely supping from her flute. George kept watching her, still unable to say anything, still unable to kindle her interest. The crackling of the log fire still filling the room with an awkward ambience.

UMBILICAL REX

ACT ONE

The curtains part to reveal a flaming stage. Two silhouettes are visible between the iron bars of a prison cell. The clunking of pistons and oil drills and lawnmowers scream all over the sombre scene from somewhere out of shot. A huge digital clock flashes above with ONE HOUR in red cyphers.

Motes of light start to illuminate the men beneath the shadows - a new-born foetus, two hours old, drags a tiny comb through his thin wispy hair. He is iridescent in the low light, a swathe of afterbirth covering the crown of his soft, swollen scalp. Outside the prison gate, two guards wearing quarantine jumpsuits wave drivers through. The smog outside possesses a supernatural quality in the shade of night.

Pan to opposite cell

Disfigured globes of moulted glass emerge from the chugging heart of a furnace in the neighbouring cell. Two workers slap on a pair of industrial gloves and stoop into a sack of dead animals. The workers begin moulding the glass into beakers.

The child watches intently, side profile.

Close up on one worker stabbing his wrench into one of the mangled corpses (which may have once been a deer or a stag) and tears it open like a busted piñata. He removes each organ with a surgeons grace and throws them into a steaming pile. The strained remains fill each beaker with droplets until full.

The machinery is deafening, a medley of hydraulic rams and pumping apparatus, bone grinders and overhead cranes. The stink of metal, of the disembowelled animal carcasses and grease trapped under the belt add to the hellish image in the prison.

Image of animal corpses

Only high protein parts off the animals are ever bought these days. People rarely eat the flesh of grazing animals or fish from the sea anymore, the real market is in vital organ manufacturing. There is no evidence that these products help build immunity to the airborne virus tearing through the city.

The worker wipes the sweat and viscera from his forehead and looks down at his overalls. He's never seen so much blood, even in his 2 decades as a corpse handler. The mass of butchered life before him has never struck the man on a compassionate level before…until now.

The other worker continues to mould each glass beakers with dead efficiency. He descends his polycarbonate visor and begins preparing the glass for sintering. The kid turns away and winces but he can still hear the awful noises of the gutting process.

A cowboy sits on the bunk opposite and starts knotting up a noose. He has dark ringlets around is eyes and his face is wrinkled and agonised like a dustbowl farmer. The industrial machinery ceases its din. Both priest and child exchange an emotionless glance.

From the aperture, we see a sulphuric monsoon is developing over the city.

The cowboy tips the bill of his hat and reads from a safety pamphlet.

 - The virus has torn through this city. A new feeling will wash over the victim like a film of hot glue - a powerful, overwhelming surge that leaves the body paralysed. Victims seem to clutch at the chest region – the heart, seemingly a fragile source of constant agony.

The cowboy gives a maniacal laugh that bursts forth from the parting of his thick fish lips like puss from a pierced pimple. He stops, suddenly tensely serious. He reads again.

- The sufferer feels moisture well under the ducts. This is a truly devastating phenomenon. Every muscle in the body succumbs to lethargy - a disease of the soul spreading like wildfire. Finally, the infected drops flat out. Dead.

The cowboy clicks his spurs and yells – Well, SH-H-E-E-I-I-T! He offers the kid a cigarette. The pink ectomorph fumbles the little white rod between his stubby finger tips before accepting the cowboy's offer of a light. The baby coughs out a plume of smoke and stares through the bars of his cell. The cowboy avoids looking at the long placenta cord dangling between the kid's legs.

Dream scene of child sliding out of his vulva confines and straight into a state penitentiary

He takes another drag from the cigarette and looks at the smouldering butt all confused. The cowboy nods, chewing on a stem of wheat. Suddenly a foul smell fills the cell. The kid adjusts his diaper and gives an apologetic face. The cowboy tries to hide his repulsion.

ACT TWO

The kid becomes increasingly bored, visibly bored. He's gotten distracted by the strange figure roaming the hall outside his cell. The cowboy sighs forlornly.

- He had a hand in bringing ya here.

- A hand?

- Sh-e-e-i-t! He considers y'all a violent and reprehensible criminal.

The cowboy gives another hideous cackle that echoes against the cells stony walls. He gestures to the pacing figure outside and asks

- What do you think about him then, the surgeon or the daddy?

The kid glares into the darkness trying to focus on any familiar contours. Suddenly the voice booms – ferocious, masculine, barely human.

- VISITOR. YOU GOT A VISITOR.

A set of keys jangle in the lock and the cell door slides open. A woman appears. She seems vaguely recognisable to the baby. She is dwarfishly short with cropped black hair and two bulging, soul hungry eyes. Her breasts are large and milk engorged. They meet the baby at eye level. He stares at the two massive, sagging bags and his stomach growls with hunger. She is diminutively small but still appears tall compared to the child sitting on his bunk. The woman squats and she smiles, revealing her advanced years. The tight flesh around her mouth cracks into a grin. She is fat too. The cowboy gets up, adjusts his waistcoat and places two hands on either side of her shoulder to turn her around. They share a wet display of affection. Having stooped to her level the cowboy is almost able to consume the woman's entire head, his jaw dislocating like a python. They reluctantly separate and, together, look down at the baby.

The woman keeps grinning, undoing her large brassier with her stare fixed. She stands before him with her huge exposed breasts. The cowboy cups her left bosom as if examining its suppleness. He seems to approve.

Outside, the agent appears displeased by this display. He punches at the bars with both boulder fists, snorting and swearing insanely. The kid looks over to the neighbouring cell at a worker doubled over in pain.

Close up on anguished face – bespectacled, fat and unshaven man wearing a boiler suit on.

A television sparks into life. The agent is calm now and soon in a fit of hysterics. A re-run of M.A.S.H is on. The industrial machinery starts up again. The cowboy flips open his pamphlet again and reads.

- The victim seems to experience arousal and an erect state, which is completely perplexing. You can almost see the brain working on a million different thoughts at one time.

Worker falls to the ground, face-down - a trail of blood dribbles visibly over his chin.

- Do you miss your momma? – the woman asks snapping the kid back to attention.

- No…

- Do you miss your God?

- No…

- Do you miss *my* God?

Disgruntled by the relentless questioning and still weighed under the anvil of injustice he's carried around his neck the duration of his short, painful life – the baby feels himself succumbing to something - the tragic parables behind those wet eyes are impossible things to conceal fully. He cries.

- Baby gonna cry?? – teases the cowboy, pretending to lasso cattle from thin air. The kid clenches his eyelids shut and bashes his rattle against the frame of his bunk. The grotesque laughter gets louder, in perfect dissonance with the clattering machinery outside and the TV's blare. They're all laughing.

The priest is laughing.

The woman is laughing.

The draped agent is laughing.

Captain Trapper is laughing.

Then there is nothing.

Fade Out…

ACT THREE

The baby opens his eyes and chokes back a hoard of tears. The cell is empty and he's all alone – stuck in silence.

His surroundings look different but he can sense something has changed within himself. He looks at his reflection in the long mirror hung against the wall. He stands tall now, wearing an ivy-league jacket and acid wash jeans. The round baby face is now angular, chiselled from muscle and jagged chunks of bone. He is so broad and tall. The kid wants to cry some more but something in him resists.

The umbilical cord is still there too, sucking tight at his belly button, draining his life source. He tries to tug it free. A desire to separate himself from what he once was is overwhelming. The more placenta he pulls out the more keeps coming – in a never ending line. He gives up after a minute or so, sitting back down on the bunk with a bundled coil in his arms. The whorls and loops of his own external organ bring a flurry of nausea to his gut. The kid ups his college blazer and rubs his hands together. The cell is suddenly freezing.

He watches as the poisonous vapour outside kills two squirrels by the roadside

Outside a figure is still wandering the shadows, only he seems much smaller in stature now. The kid can hear something – the tinkling of xylophone keys. He recognises the tune but from a long time ago. He looks down to see a tiny parade of insects marching across the floor from under his bed. He lifts his knees up to his chest in automatic fright. Upon closer inspection the marching band appear to be cockroaches. They make their way to the metal bar at the foot of the cell and pass between the gap. The digital clock chimes with "TEN MINS" – at which point the cell door slides open and the agent allows a young woman to enter.

Her face is hidden by a large wicker hat with fruit on it. She promptly removes it. The woman's face is young but chalked completely white, and her nose is long and sharp like a cone. Her eyes are murky with no sign of any pupils. When she opens her mouth to speak she has a row of crystalline fangs along the top row of her gum. The kid is quite started by her.

- Don't you remember? – the woman asks.

- No.

- You don't have much time.

- I know.

- I brought you something.

The woman hands over a handkerchief.

- Open it…

The kid cautiously unwraps the offering. He stares into his palm.

- What is this?

- Your first tooth.

He holds the tooth into the light to observe it - a sharp, pointy incisor, just like the woman's. The kid gives the woman a distrustful glance.

- Not long now – she says unhelpfully.

- Here, you can have this back.

- Put it in.

The kid looks down at the fang. With his other fingers he feels along the course of his gum line until he finds a craterous space. He lodges the tooth into the hole and the root attaches immediately.

- Take a look – encourages the woman.

He bares his teeth in the mirror and sees the fang protrude beyond all his others.

The woman appears pleased revealing her own row of impossibly sharp dentures.

- Do you know what it feels like to die?

- No.

- Are you afraid of it?

- Yes.

- Do not be afraid of dying.

- Easy for you to say.

- I have died almost a dozen times.

The boy begins weeping uncontrollably. The woman forwards a handkerchief to him. He blows his nose.

- What's wrong with you? – asks the woman.

- I'm almost 3 years old.

The woman leans in and lightly tousles the boy's hair. The agent rattles the bar with his fist and announces – TIME'S UP!

The woman gets to her feet and tells the boy to stand up. He does. She presses her lips lightly to the boy's cheek, turns and leaves. The boy can still feel the cold impression she left on his flesh minutes after she has gone. The agent appears to be entering the cell. He is as tall as the boy remembers. In his left hand is a syringe full of a yellow substance. He poises his fat finger over the plunger, ready to descend.

- First thing's first – says the agent, still hidden behind a blanket of shadow. In his right hand is a surgeons tool kit with operating tools clattering around inside.

- I'm gonna cut you off for good.

The kid becomes aware of his blood saturated connecting tube. He doesn't want to lose his placenta like this. Still, he won't put up a fight. He's paralysed by futility and fear and pure curiosity. The needle spike breaks the skin and everything becomes vividly clear...

Flames engulf the stage and the curtain drops. A young lady wearing a baby's coverall wanders onto the stage sucking ruthlessly on a dummy. She begins to orate

- I know there is nothing beneath this replicated flesh but a mass of circuitry and manmade mechanisms. What is a broken heart like? Is it similar to this virus? - A fat tumour on the left hand side, throbbing like a plate of red, wobbly jelly? Do I really aspire to this? I confess this fascination with human deterioration has escalated to near obsession.

She looks at the crowd in awe for a few moments before the brutish hand of an agent appears from the depths of the curtain and yanks her through...

Applause...

THE WATERING HOLE

Originally published in the Apocalypse Donkey Anthology

That peculiar smell of Granola and spices
    Those strange dark clouds swelling overhead
    The feel of buried bone beneath the hot sand
    Sounds of a sinister marketplace where souls are bought and sold
    The idle chit-chat of hungry monsters in cages
    The howl of wind tearing through each and everyone's heart
    Juan knew he'd arrived…

He saw the bar from the hotel window. A neon sign burning through the shadowy empire of hell – TITS AND BOOZE. Juan slid on his coat and headed to the bar leaving the hotel door wide open.

On the street-side was a woman Juan recognised. She was wearing a donkey mask and squatting over a rusty bucket. He didn't stop to check how he knew her. The woman's maternal familiarity set his teeth on edge. He barged through a cluster of immaculate yuppies on their cell phones, all wearing the same mask as the woman.

- What's tha' hurry? - Asked one yuppies, snorting through a large nostril and kicking dirt behind him with one large hind hoof.

- TITS AND BOOZE! He replied in feverish haste.

A spark of excitement danced down his spine as Juan drew closer to the bar. The humid air made breathing difficult but he was driven by an insane desire deep within himself.

The marketplace was busy with ghouls and wailing souls trapped in Gherkin jars. Juan saw a familiar man browsing over a stand of buyable body parts. He had a strange contortion of pleasure on his face as the stall owner dug a candy scoop into a load of fingertips and shovelled them into a bag for him.

- Assalaamu Alaikum, I love the smell of Salaam in the mornin'- the owner said.

The familiar face took the bag and disappeared into the blackness. A fear of being castrated sank an anchor of nausea in Juan's gut.

The destination was close, he knew it.

Almost there.

Juan could smell the beer; practically feel the pink mounds of a lap dancing broad beneath the open palms of his hands. Virtually feel the hateful penis envying stares…

The clouds parted and rain descended. Still the thick humidity hung in the air like radioactive smog. Juan had to piss. He went to relieve himself behind one of the stalls. Once the stream began to flow, Juan saw a young boy he recognised.

    He had dirty blonde hair
    So did Juan
    He had a mole on his upper lip
    So did Juan

He spoke with a lazy S and his eyes sparkled in gunmetal grey…

You get the picture…

- I don't like you, said the boy.

- Good, I never liked you either, Juan replied, shaking the last of his piss out. The boy's face twisted and he began wailing.

- This is so typical of you, accused Juan, shaking a long adult sized index in the boy's agonised face. The rain stopped. He noticed a large damp stain cover over the boy's pants.

He finally reached the watering hole.

- TITS AND BOOZE –

Juan burst through the bar door barely able to contain his excitement. But his hopes were dashed when he realised the bar was empty. There was no bar, no waiter, no pool table, no tables or chairs but most alarmingly – no tits or booze! The bar wasn't a bar at all, but an empty warehouse. He heard a whimpering child facing the corner. That familiar man who wanted him castrated had removed his donkey mask. He had no face. He stared at Juan with an expressionless slab of pink flesh. Those familiar women who both aroused him and made him feel peaceful as a child were there too, equally blurred of any distinctive physiognomy.

Like the seedy motel, Juan was faced with the familiar sound of an empty room.

Outside, he could hear and smell the same things he'd always heard and smelled.

That peculiar smell of Granola and spices

Those strange dark clouds swelling overhead

The feel of buried bone beneath the hot sand

Sounds of a sinister marketplace where souls are bought and sold

The idle chit-chat of hungry monsters in cages

The howl of wind tearing through each and everyone's heart.

- Aren't you going to take off that mask Juan, it's hardly kosher? – came a voice he scarcely recognised.

Juan knew he'd arrived…

DEEP SURGERY

OK nurse, scalpel please

Souls are difficult things to find

You know

Even for one so qualified

But I'll root around the red stuff some more

I always get my man

You know

My patients often howl for god

Even when they've been heavily sedated

I tell you

It's enough to…

10 cc's of that stuff in the jar, please nurse

Yes, the one that stored your gherkins

Fill a syringe of it

Now tweak the tip

You know how to drop the plunger don't you nurse?

7 years of training I suppose

And now stick it in my arm

That's right

These leaves of folded flesh inside this deep hole

Are enough to make you…

A pail nurse, a pail!

You know

The linoleum tiles are covered in his guts

You'll mop up later won't you?

Keep looking

The anal camera please, at once

Someone dab my brow

I'm going in

Hold my instruments

Hold my gloves

SCHADENFREUDE

You know

It's really unspectacular in here

This chap is all flesh and bone

Just bloody walls and muscular bits

Can you hear me up there nurse?

Yes, yes it's me

Of course it's me

Send down a ladder and a small team of surgeons

Yes now!

Tell them I could be trapped in here

Tell them there's nothing else

Tell them I've tried looking

Inside

WIRE AND SPITTLE

BY

CHRIS KELSO

TRACK 1#
HOW LOW CAN YOU GO?

Leatherface turned the transmitter up higher – KILLER ART COLONY were playing a song called HIGH-TECH FUK from their JOURNALISM E.P. Leatherface thrashed his head around so hard he looked like a man trying to give himself whip lash. Or someone was trying to shake themselves free of a bug infestation. A cable of veins shot up his neck and forearms as he romped around the driver's seat until a lorry beeping at him head-on forced Leatherface to re-take control of the steering wheel. He was travelling down the long tarmac artery to visit his brother's widow in Wire City. Germ had just committed suicide two days before - lost all hope when he realised the world had outgrown him. Leatherface wheeled the volume knob on the transmitter to full ear assault. The radio drooled a slur of vowels.

- CRANK IT UP!! MUTANT CUNT MUTHA FUCKA! TOURING WITH ART/ HEROIN/DEATH AT THE WIG-WAM CLUB! THIS IS THEIR NEW SINGLE WHICH IS ALSO ON FREE DOWNLOAD FROM OUR WEBSITE - FUCK ALMIGHTY-Y-Y-Y-Y!!!!!

A guitar riff thrashed through the speaker like something indistinguishable from a load of scrap metal falling into a belt sander. The singer spat out lyrics but was also known to tour with his own spoken word material from time to time. Leatherface was making his journey in a crumby fed-sled and had already removed the chrome badge from the front grill in protest. He hated brands.

He'd been in his own band once - a queer-core band called the RADICAL FAERIES whose biggest achievement was opening a band slam night for THE PINK SATURDAYS at the Subculture Club. RADICAL FAERIES were straight-edge as they came but Leatherface never really adhered to that philosophy too strictly during his time in the band. He very rarely participated in any of the gay sex either.

The motorway was long and the weather had this unique light. Battleship grey. He lit a Cap and sucked at the spool until his exhaling breath went hoarse. It felt good to be leaving Spittle Town. Felt good to leave behind the flophouses, the Freeze-dens and all the stagnant relationships that were quickly turning sour. There were no real people in the city. The beltway out of Spittle was practically empty. Maybe an existential country road-trip would do Leatherface some good.

He had an upright strip of hair from his nape across the centre of his head. He popped the glove compartment and took out a squeeze tube of superglue, squirted a spoonful into his open palm and ran it across the length of the Mohawk. He wiped the rest onto his faded, grey sweatshirt that had a picture of a suited man with a vinyl record for a head firing an AK47 into the air. Leatherface was bald on one half and used to have a swastika shaven into the left side before he covered over it himself with a circle-A. He had this scar across his cheek like it'd been dragged across the naked spike of a rusty nail. He doesn't remember how he got it. His mouth was bone dry but he ignored the urge to pull over at a gas station. Leatherface just wanted to get to Wire City.

****

He hadn't come across much in his first hour driving - sculptured dunes, some crusted salt flats, valleys, canyons, a regiment of Joshua Trees and lots of orange rocks covered in desert varnish. The giblet soups of wayside road kill. The breakers yard piled high with pancaked cars right beside the interstate and sinister capitol buildings that lurked in the downtown shadows. Hobos with Styrofoam cups full of copper...

The radio was talking again.

- *Jane from Omaha asks if we all want to be saved?*
- *What's an Omaha?*
- *Hmm...I have no idea!*

He got to thinking. Germ was dead and that was too bad but Leatherface wasn't driving all this way to see his widow just to organise a sad-ass funeral where everyone was going to be bummed out. Lonny, Germ's girl, invited the whole crew up to Scarlet House in Wire City to see his corpse one last time before they buried him. Clit. Shithead. Rubber. Vandal. The whole gang would be there. It was going to be insane. Or so he had thought.

TRACK 2#
IN SCARLET HOUSE -

Skittle was dancing to FUCK ALMIGHTY by MUTANT CUNT, stomping and punching his fists in the air. He started singing the chorus

- FUCK ALMIGHTY, FUCK ALMIGHTY, THE COMET'S COMING BUT WE DON'T CARE!

Skittle wasn't quite right in the head. Not in an anarcho-punk, anti-conformist sort of way. More like in a mentally handicapped sort of way. He was awkward and always spoke out the side of his mouth and his wrists twisted askew when he walked but he had punk in his soul so everyone thought he was cool. Maybe he just didn't know what the fuck was going on. He was never in a band himself but did some messed up album artwork for bands like NECRO, MYSTERION ICONOCLAST and SONIC VAGINA. He was probably a genius in his way, like Picasso or something (before he became a Commie poster-boy). This was his place but he probably belonged in a carnival.

Cutter appeared from behind a glass shutter. His head was shaven leaving a pepper of pinpricks over his skull. He was a tall guy, broad and swollen with muscle. Cutter hardly ever wore a shirt, just bleach spattered suspenders covered in patches and safety pins that looped over his shoulders and met in a Y-shape across his back. He wore steel toe capped army boots and followed his own strict skinhead shoe lace code - Blue to show he was a cop killer. Black to show he was fresh-cut. Green to display Celtic pride and scarlet red to show he had Nazi tendencies. His lip had a piercing needle punctured through it, erupting over with excess scar tissue. Cutter was showing off, dangling and stretching the needle up in people faces.

- You should put a Band-Aid on that.

Shithead suggested, examining the septic flesh.

- I like my cuts to bleed

- FUCK ALMIGHTY, THE COMET'S COMING BUT WE DON'T CARE!

Cutter cringed. FUCK ALMIGHTY was still booming out of Skittle's juke-box and he was still dancing around like a maniac. Suddenly aware of the attention he was drawing to himself, he stopped milling his arms around. Cutter walked heavily up towards Skittle and brought the back of his hand down onto the dancing retard. He crashed to the tarmac.

Suddenly a smell of shit grabbed at everyone's throats. If Lonny had been there Cutter wouldn't have struck Skittle but she was out picking up glue and vegetables at the grocery store so he pretty much had to fend for himself.

- I'm gonna puke. Gross!

- Skittle fuckin' shit himself!

People were gagging, punks were puking.

Cutter was hard-core through and through. He wore these studded wristbands with real clumps of jagged, rusty metal sticking out the cuff. He'd beat himself onstage like Joss State from MONKEY GLAND did. Cutter was a big fan of theirs. A *real* fan.

- Go wipe your ass you retard fuck.

- Fuck you, you macho prick.

Everyone laughed like a posse of hideous monkeys getting de-haired. When he wasn't at gigs or playing rhythm guitar/backing vocals in his own band, SHIT CAUGHT IN A PIGSTORM, Cutter was busy pumping iron and shooting his mouth off. He also ran LO-FI MUZIK production with Shithead.

****

JOSS STATE/ MONKEY GLAND

- MONKEY GLAND raped my ears! Shouts a protester. Her reply – You're lucky that's all we raped!

Joss State was lead singer for MONKEY GLAND and became infamous among underground gig junkies as something of a wild man. He was one of those tough city rats - thick haired, hard faced strong jawed, stuffed pecks. He had a truly rancid stare. Most notably remembered for his on-stage antics which included, to name a few - defecating on stage then eating it, spitting into the audience, punching people in the front row, smashing his skull repeatedly with the microphone until his face was a fractured melon of cascading blood, smashing the crowds skulls repeatedly with the microphone, raping and humiliating female audience members and kicking seven shades of shit out of anyone who spoke against him. People would turn up in their droves, often dared to attend. Almost always they'd leave covered in cuts and bruises and psychosomatic trauma that would stay with them long into adulthood. People would go to one MONKEY GLAND gig and claim they were diehard fans. That the awful behaviour and physical brutality added to their love for the band, more specifically for Joss State. But if you were a diehard MONKEY GLAND fan, I mean a real follower who went to every show like Cutter did, chances are you were someone equally as disturbed as State was and wouldn't last long in the outside world before the authorities caught you and stuck you in a padded cell.

MONKEY GLAND were a band waterlogged with conflict, often criticised for their violent gigs, vandalism, the never-ending stream of court cases, controversial album art and long stints in federal prison. While the band had its detractors they were regarded by some as a vital antithesis for ordered society and consumerism. They created media storms everywhere they went and eventually wound up getting dumped by 2 major labels.

In one infamous documentary, a small road crew followed MONKEY GLAND around the country on their POWERVIOLENCE tour in a shitty rented van. During a four month period of extensive gigging and drinking, things started to get heavy. The bus broke down 4 times and it became apparent State was succumbing to side effects of cabin fever. Becoming increasingly nihilistic, at first he just overslept all the time but his moods were to take a sinister turn. Combining this with the groups month-long narcotic consumption and gross under nourishment, State attacked and killed the band's then-lead guitarist, Rank, in the tour-bus, strangling him with a guitar lead while he slept in the bunk below. There was a popular and completely feasible rumour going around that suggested Joss State kept alive by fucking his sister and his mother without a rubber then eating the aborted foetus. The controversy didn't end there. On the final day of the POWERVIOLENCE tour a heated debate between State and a tight fisted club owner consequently ended in a broken neck and 10 broken fingers for the owner. He was also centre of an on-going murder investigation into tour manager, Salvador Props, who was found face down on a massage table, bludgeoned, stabbed 9 times and robbed of $17,000 from his wallet in The Fury Motel. There could be no bureaucracy in anarchy. Joss State was a fucking post punk myth.

ALL THOUGHT IS LIE.
ALL LOVE IS LONELINESS.
ALL HAPPINESS IS IGNORANCE

- (*MONKEY GLAND, THETRUTHABOUTU*)

TRACK 3#

The pylon wires above waved in the wind casting shadows on the sandy pavement. Leatherface drove past the famous Fury Motel in midtown and thought about Salvador Props. Props always had a seedy reputation, a product of Spittle's stinking urban hive. He was a crook. A lowlife whore. Leatherface never knew the guy personally or anything but he'd been to see RADICAL FAERIES play in Lug Nuts just before he croaked. They never got to find out what Props thought or whether he'd wanted to sign them or not but it could've been the most important day of the bands existence. In the end RADICAL FAERIES disbanded and no-one seemed to care. It was that night Joss State left him as a pound of mincemeat on the massage table - a lump of raw flesh with a screaming mouth. That was his big chance. He wasn't going to pay two grand to put himself through medical school like mom wanted. Leatherface swore revenge on State and if he ever crossed his path again he'd rip him a new asshole, legend or no legend.

He turned up the dial on his radio. Two men were having an intense debate about something.

- No, no, no! A real man jerks off into a sock he's worn all day long, tosses the sock on the floor, then wears it again the next morning. THAT'S a real man.

- NO! No, no, no…

****

In Scarlet House, an all-female band was performing a sound check. This gig was considered historic. It was the first time SCARLOT HARLOTS had played in over four years. The woman, Lyric, clutching the microphone stand was quite good looking. She started adjusting the P.A system and producing drones of - 1, 2…1, 2…3, 4…1, 2

Lyric was a bit different from the rest. She was one of the few older punk girls who hadn't ended up a washed up whore. Her band SCARLOT HARLOTS were something a bit different too. They weren't like the other bands whose only talent seemed to be combining seemingly random adjectives to form a band name. SCARLOT HARLOTS had an agenda. They thought of themselves as more of a resistance movement than a punk band. They championed animal rights and direct action and were anti everything – anti-racism, sexism, globalisation. They denounced materialism, opposed war and consumerism. They dressed collectively in military surplus clothing and had an exclusively female line-up. They played a memorable sell out gig at the Wig-Wam jazz club and sold 100,000 copies of their third single DEATH: THE SEQUEL on the same night, but never made the mainstream chart, which suited them fine. But they couldn't elude fame and acclaim no matter how hard they tried. Cue a megabucks recording contract from BLOODY EAR. Soon after the success of their gold selling third studio album W.A.R-T they quickly disappeared from the public view, squatting in a 16th century commune to recoup and were left cursing the hypocrisy of their own success. The commune became known as Scarlet House. A crash pad for fellow artists and friends, full of half pipes and collapsing, graffiti'd joists. It had a yard and a decent sized basement and an attic packed full of recording equipment. Scarlet House stood tall at 6 stories high, had 2 side wings and aside from some boarded up windows and an asbestos ceiling was in great condition.

****

Spaz was high, stumbling around the parking-lot with a Jam pipe dangling from his lips. He bounced off of cars like someone trapped inside an insane pinball arcade. When he opened his mouth his breath blasted forth like a shotgun fire of halitosis. Point blank range could melt someone's face right off. His sneakers were worn to the sole. Spaz was the most fucked up of the whole bunch when it came to Jam and alcohol. Once found in possession of what prosecutors described as - "an obscene amount of Freeze."

He approached the stage where SCARLOT HARLOTS were powering through a melancholic rendition of MY KAMASUTRA HOROSCOPE by SONIC DEATHGRIP and yelled

- KICK OUT THE JAMS MOTHERFUCKERS!

The girls kept playing. Spaz resumed his empty stare like some lobotomy patient who'd wandered out of his ward. Cutter and Scandal were laughing in the distance. Spaz picked up a bottle of stale beer that lay on the grass and drank it. It went down like a cup of warm piss but seemed to hit the spot.

Punks only really called him Spaz to be disdainful. No doubt had he avoided all this excess he would've been one of those successful geeks crunching data for the government or something. He actually had an I.Q of near genius measures and before he became a stinking punk attended Easton state university studying Physics, Mathematical Descriptions and Classic Mechanics. Fucker loved science, in particular Quantum physics. He liked to mess around with the thought of quantum suicide, placing a gun to his head and playing Russian roulette alone in the dark. He was so drunk he couldn't ever remember if he'd decided to load it. He liked to think that in one universe he was alive and in the other he could be dead what with the universe splitting every time he pulled that trigger. Being alive was just one possibility. That was his excuse, his excuse for not actually having the guts to kill himself by more conventional means. Apparently when he found out about the comet that was hurtling towards Earth he just stopped giving a rat's ass…

****

- How does that sound?
   - A bit tinny Lyric love.
   - Up the treble.
   Lyric stood back to view her band. She started murmuring numbers to herself again
   - 1, 2…

****

Vandal forked at his dick. Lonny ate out his asshole while Shithead sucked between his legs. Vandal's hole puckered. He was about to shoot. His dick tasted like a battery acid Popsicle. Callused hands streamed over Shithead's hair. Every part of Vandal was cut with thick bone that jutted out like ripe acorns under the skin. Lonny pulled away, her guts mushy with guilt. Germ had only just killed himself. What the fuck was she doing? Vandal's cum shot out like a geyser of hot rhubarb, thick and run through with blood into Shithead's face.
   - Thanks guys - Vandal said, seemingly content to lie with his pants at his ankles, covered in his own spunk.
   - Forget it. Me next time though - Lonny wiped her mouth with the cuff of her sleeve.
   - No way. I don't eat out chicks assholes.
   - After what I just did for you?
   Vandal shrugged.
   - I'd be expecting you to suck my lungs out after the rim job I just fucking gave you!
   - Sorry. Vandal shrugged again.
   Shithead clambered to his feet and stretched. He spat out a clot of Vandal's cum.
   - I only fuck chicks. In the pussy you know?
   - Charming.
   - I'll fuck your pussy Lon. Vandal offered.
   Shithead got involved.
   - You should write poetry.
   - Fuck you. Vandal was now pulling up his pants and buckling his jeans over.
   - You kiss your mother with that mouth?

- No, but I sure kiss yours good with it, fruitcake.

They all laughed. Shithead's face screwed up in concern suddenly.

- You should get yourself checked down there.

- Yeah, a lotta blood today. Lonny clarified.

- I can get it checked anytime man.

- You'll regret it.

- Ain't got no time for doctors man.

- Why?

- I got Germ's funeral then I got a gig to prepare for in a week. No time for mother fucking scalpel jockey.

- Where's the gig?

- Blue-Collar Ridge man. First we're gonna cut through Easton. Last time we were there we terrorised that little college town. The kind of town that pisses me off, you know? The kind where every mother fucker drives a bicycle and wears a back-pack.

- What you gonna do?

- Cloudy got this jar of bees. We gonna let it loose into the crowd man. Watch those student fags fucking squirm. Root out the filth.

He glared at the ground, at the abattoir-worth of blood that he'd just expelled from his penis and frowned.

- Shit. That's a lot of blood huh?

TRACK 4#

Leatherface's skin felt tight with the cold that desert nights often brought. He was still a little goof-balled from smoking all that Freeze. It had been so piping hot that day he couldn't quite believe the dramatic shift in temperature. Earlier he'd filled the car up with gas and could barely touch the bodywork. Now all the metal on the interior was freezing. Lex ended things with Leatherface. Jerked him around. Burnt his heart like it was made from matchsticks. He couldn't allow himself to think about that. Not now. That's the danger with long drives - the constant motion and alone-time means these thoughts can breed and just thinking about it tied knots in his gut.

The tank was running low again. He'd just went past a sign saying the next station was only a couple of miles further West - Blue Collar Ridge.

The gas station was called SKUNK'S and looked like a shitty little shack with a couple of gas dispensers plotted in the sand out front like crooked gravestones. Leatherface got out, filled his car with gas and went into the shack to buy something to eat.

He swaggered down the aisles with an armful of gas station junk - bubble gum, candy bars, cans of soda and discount beer and one porn magazine. He dumped the crap onto the clerks counter. The clerk looked like a real redneck and didn't take his eyes off of Leatherface while he scanned each item. In the store-room, his boss-eyed daughter piled boxes and an older guy drank from the pale-gold body of a beer bottle. He rang it all up. The register ka-chinged.

- 20 bucks.

Leatherface rooted around in his jeans but could only find bottle caps and zip-loc bags, back and front. He filled his cheek with his tongue trying to be playful.

- This is embarrassing.

The redneck just stared.

- Could I send you a cheque or something pal? I'll leave you my details?

The redneck gave a wry smile, lowering his shoulder and placing his fingertips on the butt of a shotgun that rested under the counter. Leatherface raised both hands on reflex.

- Hey pal. You've had yourself a long night. Take a walk around the block. Walk it off huh?

The gun was now cocked with Leatherface staring down the barrel.

- Yoor ki'a scum make me sick.

The white trash daughter was taking notice. The old guy still drank from his bottle. Leatherface didn't even flinch. The shotgun was filthy and it was obvious from how he held it that the guy hadn't had to use it much, even if he'd been seemingly waiting for this opportunity to arrive for a long time. He saw the redneck load the wrong calibre ammo and knew it would backfire.

****

Cutter swaggered into the pit of punching punks. He raised two meaty palms in the air and told everyone to shut the fuck up for a sec. They did.

- We got a special guest coming soon.

People began to murmur.

- The great Joss State will be gracing us with his presence tomorrow night. He's been convinced to do a 5 song set on New Year's Eve.

Everyone started cheering and freaking out. People were hugging each other as if Jesus were stopping by to bless their foreheads or something. Vandal, Shithead and Lonny shared kisses and hugs. Every punk was ecstatic. Everyone except Lyric that is. She knew SCARLOT HARLOTS slot would get sacrificed. She knew MONKEY GLAND would play well over their given slot. This was supposed to be her comeback gig not some limp dick fascist murderer's. In her own home too…

- This news will define us! Yelled Spaz who was ignoring his body's scream for liquor and his hungry veins. Tonight he'd get chalked up good on Jam caps. The chronic dependency for Freeze had left Spaz with buckshot eyes and he was fast turning ghostly white. Some dread-head came up behind him and kissed Spaz on the neck, a gesture he seemed not to appreciate. Lyric stormed up to Cutter and led him to the side. Her face all holier-than-thou.

- What's up with you? You look like you've been eaten by a wolf and shat over a cliff edge!

- So DEVILS DANDRUFF won't be supporting anymore?

- What?

- They were chosen to support us because they shared our philosophy. They won't want to share the stage with those Nazi fucks.

- And you guys do?

- This is our gig. MONKEY GLAND aren't ruining this night for us. We won't be pressured out of our slot. This is our home. Joss State isn't welcome.

- Well I'm the promoter and I been your shitty band babysitter on plenty of occasions. Today I say they play. It's too big to shun man!
- You're full of shit.
- Look, we got some Pop and some Kool-Aid fresh in. Why don't you take a blast…?
- Forget it. Not interested.

Cutter scratched his huge bicep and smeared a crudely etched tattoo of a Nazi sun wheel.

- Where are all the heroes huh?

****

APOLITICAL were playing their slot with great fervour. A small crowd of die-hard fans had even gathered before the stage. Clay pigeons starting catapulting through the air (That was Cutters idea). Lead singer, Weasel, got handed a boomer and looked like he was about to aim for the target but turned the gun on himself instead. Shithead and Vandal managed to wrestle it out of his hands in the nick of time. A stray bullet fired into an amp sending sparks of exploding circuitry onto the face of APOLITICAL'S Jewish drummer, Kris Krist Killer. In the end Krist Killer had to return to the city after part of his face was hideously burned in the accident. Skin was grafted back on, taken from his chest and his inner thigh.

TRACK 5#

The rednecks headless body lay dangling over the counter. His fingers still loosely hung around the shotgun trigger while blood spouted out an artery. His daughter and the old drunk looked at Leatherface as if this were all his fault. So what? Another hick bit the dust. A fucker so *right* he'd practically fallen off the plane. The old goober stood up, throbbing with vengeance and told the girl to go start up the fucking truck. She did. Tooled up in a plaid flannel shirt and acid wash, he cut an impressive picture for one so old. Now he was standing up, Leatherface could see his beefy build, strong as an ox. Greyed mullet tails down either side of a trucker cap. Classic white trash. He gave a sick, mean expression. Leatherface ran.

The desert went on for miles. Nothing but endless orange sandbanks. There was no reception out this far from Spittle, only shitty motown radio stations.

Back home he'd held down an ok job as a cabby. It had long hours and the pay sucked but it was something. More than he had now. He was entering Wire's outskirts and leaving Blue Collar. Thank fuck he thought, almost there. Concrete started appearing. Sand piled up to the curb. Leatherface gave a thin smile to himself…

****

Judge and Doughboy were enjoying the gig and high on the knowledge that Joss State was coming to town in time for Germ's big send-off. Judge was an old fashioned cowboy type. He wore these freshly laundered rhinestone shirts and had spurs on his mukluks but he was old school punk too. Doughboy was just a kid, wore the same Notre Dame hoody all the time and had a buzz cut. He always looked beat. Robbed of sleep. That's what Pop'll do to you. They leaned over the mezzanine looking down at the Scarlet House main-stage. In the distance was uptown Wire City, the place they'd all fled. Even from the spot on the mezzanine you could see the rain slicked highways. See the Day-Glo of 24 hour dime stores and storefronts. Smell the fried grease. Mole people living in the subway shafts and under the sewers. See the filth in the gutter, on the sidewalk. They belonged there. But they couldn't go back. Not ever.

Clit was on the can when the bathroom door swung open. A punk called Zeke stumbled in, ran up to the sink and started belching over it - these obscene vowels.
- BWAAAAAA - *oh my god* - BAAARRRRPPP - *I'm gonna puke…*
- GET THE FUCK OUTTA HERE ZEKE YOU ASSHOLE IM TRYIN' TO TAKE A SHIT!
Spaz felt he deserved a few minutes alone to veg out. He took a toke of Freeze. He felt his soul warm and his brain being drilled as the Jam Cap gently kneaded his heart and mind, bathing all his problems in green acid. Suddenly Shithead ran into view screaming and shouting something.
- JENKINS! FUCKIN JENKINS IS HERE!
Doughboy screwed up his eyes
- Is that Shithead?
Judge couldn't tell.
- What's he saying?
Cutter stuck his head round the corner of the patio door, sweating and out of breath
- It's Jenkins…
- Jenkins?
- Fucking scatter. Tell the rest. Scatter. Go.
Judge and Doughboy bolted back into the house.

JENKINS

- A raw male force that prowled Wire's theatre district, beating up punks, bums and hookers. He was an animal. His flat face, snub nose and absence of a neck gave Jenkins this inhuman look. His eyes were dead and he had this long hair that fell over the left side of his face making him look like some sick-o drag queen. He could walk through walls, carried a cannon strapped his waste nicknamed "Buck Jr" and he threw his baton around with reckless abandon - the T-1000 of the Wire City police force. He was determined to clean up his town but he was no boy scout.
And here he was, drooling like a crazed schizoid, tubes and vessels poking out his neck. Fresh herpes ulcer above his lip. He'd never been to Scarlet House before. Never this far into the punk's safety zone. This wasn't his territory. No one was ready for this. Jenkins strolled into the garden swinging his weapon into the faces of helpless punks - some who were just sitting reading or sun-bathing. One couple got hit unexpectedly just as their tongues locked in a pretzel shape. The whip of his cosh echoed. The hollow crack of the bat upon contact with a skull made sick mushy sounds. This was a fucking massacre. Bones cracked like a carrot being crunched by a noisy eater. Shithead, who'd seen him coming first, got struck on the back of the head for his trouble. He doubled over and puked onto his hands. Cutter had a shooter but had seldom used it and Jenkins managed to knock it clean out of his hand, breaking the wrist. He

brought a patrol boot down onto Cutter's neck and stamped. Hard.

- YOU LUCKY AH DON'T BRING BUCK JOONIA OUT TA PLAY YOU FUCKIN FREAKS!

People were screaming like crazy. Skittle got hit so hard it might've just cured his brain. Most had the presence of mind to leave the premises but some were determined to go down with their ship. The lawn was covered in blood and puke and people sprawled out flat face-down. Lonny got herself almost smacked into a coma for trying to protect Germ's open casket. Jenkins coughed up a spit-wad onto Germ's corpse.

- GOOD RIDDANCE TA YA FREAK!

Saps who'd tried just hanging out in the lobby, hoping Jenkins wouldn't come inside got a surprise when he appeared in the archway pirouetting his cosh. Lyric and the rest of SCARLOT HARLOTS made for the attic full of recording equipment. It had a double-lock door and Jenkins wouldn't be able to get in. So they thought. He materialised in the landing covered with blood like a butcher fresh from the farmyard shift - drips of dark, red punk guts dripping from his weapon. Under his arms were damp pit stains. The girls ran upstairs but Jenkins managed to grab the leg of Lyric and pulled her back down.

- YOU GOIN DIE MISSY!
- YOU'RE FULLA SHIT COPPER!

He dropped his bat onto her face.

- CHEW ON THIS WHORE!

Lyric bit her tongue and spat the blood onto the cops uniform. This pissed Jenkins off. She somehow managed to kick him away and headed to the bathroom but he slid the cosh under her advancing foot and she fell head first into the faucet. The girl laid there, a rag of skin flapping around like a soggy comic book. Lyric's blood glistened like crystal as Jenkins cuffed her limp wrist to the rail of the bathtub. Lyric wouldn't get back up.

- ITS TIMES LIKE THIS MUTHAFUCKAZ THAT I BE GLAD THEY'A COMET A'COMIN TO WIPE Y'ALL OFF THIS HERE PLANET…

The cop started smashing the place up eliciting screams from the attic. Jenkins kicked over a TV planted on an egg crate. More screams.

- COME OUT COME OUT… He taunted.

Drum symbols crashed noisily to the floor as they all tried to cram into the tight space full of equipment.

Jenkins was obviously trying to make lieutenant.

Disaster. Clouds ghosted over the sky like rotted marshmallow fluff.

****

Back in Wire City, Jenkins was feeling pretty pleased with himself. He helped himself to a bagel and gave the vendor a buck. Jenkins started scoping out a suspicious looking creep buying fruit at the deli.

- Got any Calzone? - Asked the creep who had a champagne coloured tan and a tight white t-shirt on.

- What you see is what I got - said the vendor.

- Dollars to donuts I can knock you over in one punch.

- You break it you pay for it.

- Calzone?

- Hey scooch, this is a fuckin deli. Ya dig?

Jenkins waltzed over and flashed his badge. Sensing things were about to kick off he pulled out Buck Jr for effect. The creep and the deli vendor started sniffing the air as if they could smell a stinking pig.

- I SEEN FUCKIN CUM SACKS WASH UP ON WIRE BEACH SCARIER THAN YOU FUCK 'EDS. Jenkins started shining the nozzle of his cannon with a handkerchief.

- WANNA GO DOWNTOWN CREEPAZOID?

- No officer - Said the creep with the champagne tan.

- SAUERKRAUT, MAYO AND A FRANK. PUT THEM ON A BUN.

The vendor started picking out what Jenkins wanted with intricate care.

- Yes officer.

Jenkins was preparing to drag him back to the station anyway when he spotted a kid racing by on a bicycle. Jenkins's teeth clenched together and he got that angry sweat coming on whenever he caught injustice red handed. His pits leaked. He reached for Buck Jr and took aim…

****

Leatherface slowed down the car outside a tough looking residential neighbourhood. Some guy was screaming at a drugstore clerk to fill his fucking bag with pills. Kids were running wild on the streets and gunshots rang from every block. He was relieved to see a face he recognised. A black dude was laying up a perfect shot in the basketball court. Spook. Leatherface was on good terms with Spook and met him through driving the cabs from Spittle to uptown Wire. He stank like a skunk but then he did live amongst trash these days. They found Spook's brother stuffed in a dumpster with a plastic bag pulled over his head and a gunshot wound to the throat. An enforcer they said. The kid wouldn't touch a fly. Jenkins hated punks and niggers. Spook was as black as they came, like a Three Musketeers bar dipped in road tar then wrapped up in carbon paper. Beautiful colour. He had an afro and a hoody with a beat-box on it. His teeth were jagged and rotting as if he'd entered into a rock-eating contest and won. A stereo sat on a melon crate pumping out black poetry. Spook was one of the few good ones left. Leatherface couldn't contain his grin. Spook came out the court and leaned himself on a hydrant that was leaking a little water. Leatherface hooked his fingers in the mesh cage.

- Mother fucker…

- Hey Spook

- Wa's happnin man?

- Finally got out huh?

Spook nodded. He'd been sent to prison for vandalism. Terrible things happened to him there. He came out a gentler person though.

- You *still* working in Wire?

- Tryin' to.

- Cab driving?

- Nah, hung it up man.

- Why you still here?

- Hacking out my novel man.

- And money?

- Grub it. Or workin on the Scow. A garbage barge transportin'trash from Wire to Blue Collar.

Leatherface tried to hide how lame an idea he thought writing a novel was the best he could and spat onto the hot macadam.

- So a novel huh? Neat idea.

- S'right! When the comet hits Earth you better bet you sweet ass I ain't gonna be remembered for workin' on no mother fuckin garbage dump. You dig?

He gave a wise old stare like someone who knew. Like someone who'd been given a lethal dose of reality. A taxi dispatcher, broad, tank-topped with gym pants on, yelled from his booth curb-side.

- THAT ONE, HEY MOTHER FUCKER YOU DEAF? TAKE THAT ONE!

A shish kebab wagon stank up the streets. The distraction of the screaming, stinking commotion was tough to take. Spook sighed.

- The comet! PFFFT! How long until our brains get turned to Jell-O and were getting barcodes on the back of our necks scanned for identification?

- I guess.

- How's you and Lex?

- Over.

- Shit. Germ OK?

- Um, he's dead Spook. Didn't you hear?

- Shit. Cops?

- No. Took his own.

- I dig, I dig. Shit's startin' to get heavy. Lotsa decent folks be killin' themselves man. Comet n'all. Sorry to hear bout Germ man. He was a good guy. Good punk.

- Jenkins been roaming?

- He's always roaming.

- Got a feeling he won't be happy to see me.

- I'll keep chicky for 'em man.

- Thanks Spook.

He looked at Leatherface with sympathy on his mind.

- Here man.

Spook produced some money from his back pocket.

- I got plenty man.

The bills lay fanned out between Spooks fingers in front of him. Leatherface thanked his friend for always being there when he needed him.

- Buy yourself a six of beer buddy.

A cop siren hastened Spook's transferring over of the cash. They parted ways.

TRACK 6#

A liquor store thief whizzed past Leatherface with a canvas bag full of clinking bottles. Wire was becoming more crazy. More like Spittle. The punk scene was dying off here and replacing itself with street scum. He couldn't wait to reach Scarlet House. But he had some money now and needed to eat bad.

Leatherface was walking down the sidewalk, a street called Kowalski Green, thinking things were going ok considering the rep he and his brother once had in these parts. Steam rose up through vents creating fog while sparks of electricity flickered from an open fuse box and he could still feel the sand gathered up in his boots. He checked out his Mohawk in a storefront window and felt good about things. Until suddenly Leatherface felt hands seizing him, covering over his mouth and pulling him into an alleyway.

It was just a bunch of mullet heads but one of them had a knife. Pinned against the brick wall, they all moved closer to him like a kindergarten class full of nightmarish yard-apes. If he wasn't mistaken one of them was beating himself off. One boy spat on Leatherface's sneakers and told him to hand over all his money but Leatherface pleaded with the kids that he left his wallet at home. Which he had.

- Listen to this pussy blubbering for his momma!
They all laughed. The main kid shoved his mush into Leatherface's.
- You think I look like a kid? Like a fucking sap, huh bitch? I'm fresh outta high school! We woulda all been going to Easton university too. What you think oh that?

Two of the kids started rooting around Leatherface's jeans and jacket for cash and found the 10 dollars 50 cents Spook loaned him. He thought that even with all the cockroaches and bullshit and crime and crooked cops and druggy lowlife's in Wire City, it didn't even compare to how bad his hometown of Spittle was.

- THIS BITCH AIN'T GOT NO CLOTHES WORTH STEALIN'!

The boys thought Leatherface's clothes were worthless because he had removed all the brand names in protest. He hated brands. Leatherface caught sight of the boy's cardboard den. This seemed to aggravate them. The kid with the knife seemed weak and skinny but saw fit to cut Leatherface across the cheek. He was sure now that the kid toward the back was jerking off - his dick like a small, fat gherkin. Someone clocked him hard over the head with a backhander sending him careening into a trashcan. Then the main kid picked Leatherface up, kicked him up the ass and pushed him off back into the street.

- Stay away from uptown you bum. Yelled a pip-squeak thug.
- You ain't welcome here freak.
- I rip out ya fuckin spleen!

It started to rain. Leatherface looked up at the pylons and streetlamps as night fell. The water stung his freshly cut cheek. His Mohawk was now flat and fine as spaghetti because of the rain.

A hobo sat on the street outside the pharmacy, soaked in rain water. He was wearing paint stained over-all as if he'd just been decorating apartments or something. He had no legs and sat in a cart holding a placard that read - GOD SENDS COMETS TO TEACH US LESSONS!

Noticing Leatherface reading his board, the bum flipped the sign over. It said - QUEERS AND FAGGOTS RUINED WIRE. MONEY PLEASE?

Leatherface slid off a sneaker and tipped it upside down. He watched as orange sand spilt out and made a miniature dune on the sidewalk. Man did he need to eat bad.

SCHADENFREUDE

****

SPOOK

- The woman behind the kiosk handed me money from the till. She looked a bit unhinged man, with her chaotic grey hair and those deranged eyes fluttering about like she had dust trapped under the lids. She should be in here not me. Her mouth burnt into a frown. What could have made her that unhappy? It seemed like her cheek muscles hadn't ever been worked. The bitch was making me nervous. I snatched the money and left as rudely as I could manage. It's people like her that should be locked up in here. Not me.

The apartment blocks reflected in the murky lake on the outer fringes. Monochrome buildings were everywhere. A dude called Fats sat on the embankment, tugging at a fishing line. It was all his fault. Spook just snapped.
- Just push him! They said.
- Do it pussy!
- That's the cunt that called you a black bastard.
- A nigger!
- Fuckin do it.
- Do it!
- DO IT!
- DO IT!
- The mother fucker!
- **Fine**…
Big splash…

In prison Spook sat in his small bed. He hadn't moved in 40 minutes, just sat there with his elbow resting on his knee and his forehead rested on his clenched fist. Spooks eyes were shut and his mouth gave an agonised groan as he contemplated everything.
Spook lifted up his legs and lay back on the bed. His eyes were wide open now. Staring at the ceiling. A fly trapped in the cell buzzed like the noise of a million lawnmowers in summer. His shirt was unbuttoned and his nipples shrivelled up in the damp coldness piercing in through the bars. The cold made his skin turn from black to a light carbon. Spook's face was so skinny, like he'd been sucked dry by a hideous overgrown leech. His ribs were accentuated by the compression of his belly - 24 sharp bones of a cage. Spook turned on his side. Rubbing the nape of his neck he focused his eyes on the bottom corner of the room. The un-flushable stainless steel commode overflowing with piss and shit. Not that he needed to shit that much. Not with the food in there. Prison - the black hole of Calcutta only more crowded. A tiny square mirror, chipped and rusted round the edges reflected a quarter of his brow back at him.
- **They think anything black can't be trusted. It's everywhere. Can't escape it. Not in Wire. Black sheep - outcast. Black market - illegal goods trade…plenty of time to hack out my fuckin novel I guess**…
Spook stood up. He went over to the wall, crouched and stood on his head. The hard stone beneath his skull felt like it was ready to crush over it. He tried steadying his legs. The blood rushed to his face. From the tips of his toes all the way to his brain. A turned hourglass.

The buzzing of the fly stopped. It was replaced by gushing blood flowing through his ears, thundering like rapids. Spooks eyes began to roll. His skull strained under the weight of his body. The thundering of blood grew louder. He tried to gulp but he was upside down so the spittle ran out of his mouth and up his nose instead of travelling down the throat. His teeth clenched. Clench. His face ready to burst with blood. Clench. Until his arms caved and he flopped onto his side. The internal buzzing went on for another minute and then he could suddenly only hear the fly. Pressure restored itself. Became regulated. Spook wiped away the spit. A guard battered the cell door and shouted

- GET UP NEGROID. YOU'RE GOIN HOME

Walking through the sidewalk with his gym bag slung over a shoulder. A Freeze Cap burning between his lips. A crucifix medallion swinging around his neck. Still as skinny. Holy denim jeans. A window shopper. An aimless stroller of high streets. What would he do now he was out? Spook knew that when you'd been locked away for a decent length of time that the outside world seemed more like prison than actual prison itself. He'd never see his buddies again but that was his decision. It was their fault in the first place. He'd read too many books in jail to know better now.

- **The man who come visit me in my dreams wears absolute darkness for a cape. I could never see his face, only two chrome eyes. He ghosts into my room in the heart of my dreams and turned them into nightmares. His hands were stone cold and its obvious blood didn't run through him and never had either. It's hard to talk about. He started coming when I was at my worst. When other kids used to abuse me. I felt so alone. My mom used to leave me alone all the time. She'd tell me she'd only be gone 5 minutes and most of the time only ever came back because I held her cigarettes and Freeze. Black dog bias - where dogs with dark coats are given for adoption in favour of those with lighter furs. The man in my dreams. Someone that couldn't be undreamt. I'm glad the comets coming. Then the fucker might leave me alone.**

He thought about getting out of Wire. Fleeing to Cowhide, Katzberg or Spittle or something. Or Vance. They don't even need to lock their doors over there. Apparently anyway. He was stuck here for now though. Glued to this place. Spook saw one of his old cab driver buddies outside the drugstore. Andy Gallaher. Junky lowlife. Got Spook into all kinds of shit as a teenager. It's clear Andy still used. His face was still strung out and any vein he had to offer was bruised with mainline markings. But Spook stops to greet Andy anyway. He was too polite in some ways.

- Finally out killer? Ha, ha! Gallaher cackled as if to suggest he'd played some part in Spooks release.

I suddenly wanted to be alone, so I shook his hand and sped off down the street and round the corner. I was out of breath, my heart pounding like angry knuckles on a door. Andy fucking Gallaher. A paranoiac state overcame me. That's the thing about being black skinned. About living in this city man and being a city boy. It's like I can't be both. But I can. I am both. Catching my breath, I tried to forget about Andy Gallaher but I'm still wired. Squeezed like a tumour between sheer fear of loneliness and a desire for immediate isolation. Shit. Can't afford to associate with my past, with fuckers like Andy. Andy's girl's a Jew. In a sense, historically, she's as persecuted as me. She's from a well-connected Jewish family. Some cunts just land on their feet. He'll never change. He won't have to cos he'll never get caught. Judaism. A dumb religion. Aren't they all? If were not

killing gays and blacks were mutilating each other's genitals with a scalpel. I went home and reamed off a torah of toilet paper.

A priest discussed Immortality of the soul. Spook found all this a bore. The guy he pushed into the river had that coming. Fats or something? Rough family. Quick to rise. Loud mouths. Black abscesses all over them. Then there was that fuck, Andy Gallaher. The voice that ushered him on. The voice that ruined his life. That Jewish bitch he was banging. A lovely looking girl. Gallaher and Fats were the same person to Spook. What was there to like about that?

In lock-up Spook read all kinds of books. Books about colonialism and renaissance art and Victorian aristocracy. Any shit they had in the prison library. Things must've been so dull in those days he thought. No punk, no rave, no rap, no decent movies, nothing. Probably why everyone took so much opiate. To escape the pain of living.

A little kid at the time. The man led me into the toilet. I lost my mom. I couldn't find her anywhere see. She should've been back in 5 minutes but she never did come back. The man led me and paid the 20 cents at the bus station toilet. We went through the turnstile and I started to panic man. He had me by the wrist, clutched real tight. There were other men in the toilet, pissing in the urinals, some in the cubicles. I relaxed. The man who'd led me in here wouldn't do anything weird in front of a load of pissing witnesses. The man found a vacant cubicle and pulled me in with him. He slid off his jacket then grabbed me by the collar and lifted me up against the wall. Shit man. He was so strong. I weighed nothing to him. Fucking nothing. My mom should've been back for me. Five minutes she says. The guy unbuckled his belt. God it was awful. Fucking awful what he asked me to do. Five minutes she says…

Can't tell if this was just a dream or not. I'm in the ocean. I'm a bad swimmer in this dream. The water was like a mirror - clear, pure. But night fell and the water ceased its transparency. I was drowning in ink. Thick waves of the stuff. The guy in the cape was there. Five minutes she says.

The surf breaking over the rocks. The cliff edge looking out to vast ocean. Oceans that led to nowhere…

****

- RETURN OF AN OLD UGLY I SEE! - Bellowed an unwelcome, familiar voice. Leatherface stood up and saw that across Kowalski Green was a cop staring at him. Jenkins. His face red as a pork chop, grinning maniacally and ready to reach for his cosh. The bum with the placard wheeled himself away down the street crying that Satan was back, Satan's back! Leatherface stood staring at Jenkins for a moment then darted back towards the alley where he'd just been mugged. Jenkins followed as fast as his stubby legs could carry the 20 stone bulk.

- NO POINT A'RUNNIN SON!!

Leatherface jumped over a fence and into the backlot. He started across yard fences behind the local YMCA where all the little deviant cockroach kids leaned out the window and started pawing and spitting vicious insults at him. Dumb puppet-headed kids. He swung from a stairwell and dropped into a piece of dumping ground where chemical drums and puddles of yellow-green scum lay everywhere. A lake of sludge almost made him lose his footing. Majestic and ugly, these were landscapes that didn't warrant a second's glance for Leatherface who'd grown up in similar holes in downtown Spittle. Jenkins was plodding not far behind.

- WAIT UP FREAK!

Leatherface couldn't catch his breath. Sweat covered his body as rain pissed down from Shangri-La. The excitement of the chase gave him extra energy to run.

Jenkins was panting loudly; he wouldn't be able to keep going much longer. Leatherface could smell the river up by the harbour. He was leaving Wire city's mainland hub, away from Scarlet House. Leatherface knew he had to lose the cop somehow and once he'd reached the port he dived straight into the murky water and swam underneath the pier's boardwalk. After a couple of minutes Leatherface heard the heavy footsteps of Jenkins thudding around up above and saw through the slats of wood the pig's bemusement and confusion. A crack of thunder and the sky went purple. An evening of wintry suburbia, an open hell-mouth. Eventually Jenkins left and Leatherface, sodden and bloody, swam to shore. Swimming was just like life. It had all the same basic principles - keep your head up, kick your legs away from the current and try not to drown...

****

BLOODY EAR STUDIOS, FLOOR 6

The secretary leaned down so far to pick up a pen, her ass stuck in his face and he almost penetrated the girl with his nose. Her dress was tight and she looked good - young, firm, fit. John Ghoul, the music agent, suddenly got a call from a client. He dismissed the secretary and picked up the receiver. People pressed their ears to the door.

- *I killed someone...* Trembled a gruff voice down the phone.

- What? Razor? Is that you?

- *Yes.*

- How are you?

- *Bad.*

- Why?

- *A journalist, I killed a journalist.*

- Thank God for that.

Ghoul gave an audible sigh of relief.

- *Eh?*

- I thought you'd gone and done something utterly immoral for a sec there.

- *But I've still killed someone John.*

- Don't worry about it. You've always been a klutz. They're not real people remember. Fascist loudmouths. Leeches. They don't care about anyone, that's what they're paid for. So don't worry about any backlash. They don't even care for their own in that business.

- *But what should I do?*

- First thing - lighten up. Now. Do you have a bathtub?

- *Several why?*

- Good. Get yourself down to D-I-WIRE and buy a canister of corrosive acid. Easy. Keep me posted.

Ghoul slammed the phone back onto its hook. He whistled and his secretary toddled back in.

TRACK 7#

RATIONAL SUICIDE - Turn your life around 180 degrees was the book Germ had been reading on the morning he killed himself. When Lonny was out, he knew exactly what he wanted to do and how. Not many people realised but his decision had been made much earlier. Lonny left Germ unaware he wanted to die. He was good at hiding that kind of stuff even from those who thought they knew him best. By 9 o'clock, Wednesday morning Germ was gone. Lonny returned to Scarlet House, where the two had been living, to find her husband with his head buried deep in the oven and the gas turned way up. She ran downstairs in a blind panic to inform Lyric who then helped Lonny remove Germ's corpse from the oven and call the ambulance. His suicide note was short

I'm killing my mind because my mind has been killing me. Shit to anyone who judges me posthumously because you can all go to hell for all I care. Lonny I know you'll understand

Love, Germ

That's the thing about these towns - the whores and roaches and lowlifes prosper while good, honest, innocent people die in the gutters, broke and forgotten for no good reason.

****

Lonny and Leatherface used to fuck. Before all of this. Before Germ went and killed himself. Fucked as in, Lonny sat on his face a few times and that was it. Fucked as in she'd tasted his dick and tickled his nuts. Never any penetration. It kept the whole thing innocent. No guilt attached without penetration.

Leatherface was heading towards her dad's old apartment. He figured she'd be cooling off there before the burial.

Leatherface rapped on the door with his knuckles. He stood in the landing waiting and looked at his hands. They were covered in cuts and tears and blossomed with deep bruising. It was only now he realised his fists were throbbing at the nub. The door opened as far as the chain would allow and the cowering silhouette of Lonny appeared. She had a Band-Aid wrapped round her head like a blood stained turban.

- Lonny. It's Leatherface.

Leatherface could hear her sniffing.

- Come on Lonny. What's the matter?

- Are you alone?

- Sure I am. What's going on?

The door swung open and she yanked him into the apartment and slammed it shut, frantically tying up the safety chain.

- What the hell happened to your head?

Lonny didn't answer. She turned to meet Leatherface and saw that he'd been cut and that he was soaking wet.

- Come on. Get out of those clothes.

She tossed him a towel and he stripped down to dry himself.

- You hungry?

Leatherface lit up.

- Oh Lonny, you got no idea how hungry I am!

She smiled and started cutting up slices of bread for him. Then her mood returned to its graveness.

- Everyone's dead Leatherface…

He stopped rubbing himself with the towel.

- What the fuck you talking about?

- They're dead. Lyric, Cutter, Vandal, Shithead. All of 'em.

- But… how?

- Jenkins.

Leatherface stood, his jaw unlatched in shock. He couldn't process all this. Outside was the skyline of tenement blocks tied together with railway line. The ocean glittered in the distance. The desert landmass beyond that. And just the vaguest impression of Spittle town's high-riser's beneath Wire's cornrose heaven. Leatherface slumped onto the sofa, naked to the waste. He felt disembowelled. Emptied. His head swam in drunken grief. Light-headed but heavy bodied. His hands numbed to physical pain. Then a lump in his throat formed and Leatherface only just managed to choke it back down. Lonny sliced up lettuce and put a wedge of ham on top then closed over the sandwich. She offered it to Leatherface but he didn't respond.

- You said you were hungry.

- I'm not anymore.

She dropped herself on the sofa beside him.

- Jenkins saw me today. Said Leatherface.

- Did he follow you here?

- Don't think so.

- I'll take your clothes to the Laundromat downstairs later.

Leatherface forced a smile of appreciation. He noticed the clogged trash chute and sighed.

- Let me get you some gauze for that cut.

As Lonny went to stand up Leatherface hung onto her belt buckle. She was a beautiful girl. Persian skinned. Her hair was electric blue and she'd done all her tattoos by herself. She was wearing a string vest that her tits were visible through. Her face looked fragile but she could kick most men's asses. She slid off her rotting plimsolls and sat back down.

- I should have never left the squat house. I shouldn't have left you and Germ.

Leatherface wanted something to happen. They both needed the comfort. Tension was thick in the air. They got fried on Freeze and fucked on the sofa then fell asleep in each other's arms. The Freeze helped. Lonny acquired a fuckload of the stuff during her time at Scarlet House.

****

- KNOCK. KNOCK. KNOCK.

Leatherface sat bolt upright.

- Who the fuck is that?
- KNOCK. KNOCK. KNOCK. KNOCK. OPEN UP!
Lonny's expression was the most sober she'd ever looked.
- PLEASE. I NEED SOMEONES HELP!
- Do not fucking answer it. Warned Lonny but Leatherface shushed her and inched towards the door.
- IT'S MY MOMMY! PLEASE.
It was definitely a young male voice. Leatherface spied through the peephole and saw some little snot-nosed kid, maybe 12 or 13. He went to unlock the door but someone forced it open from the outside, snapping the chain right off. A bunch of street kids holding pipes waltzed on into the apartment like they owned the fucking place and introduced themselves as old friends. One kid swaggered up to Lonny and grabbed her by the tit. She punched his hand away just as Leatherface was preparing himself to advance on the kid. Two other mulletheads were raiding the fridge and all the cupboards, dropping stuff on the floor deliberately. We're your worst nightmare - said the main kid who'd grabbed Lonny's tit. It wasn't the same hoods that mugged Leatherface in Kowalski Green and stole his 10 dollars 50 cents. But they were of a similar age. These kids were just as young and it didn't seem that anything was capable of scaring them. Free of fear. Hostile aliens attacking a trapped family inside their farmhouse. Cattle for the slaughter. A gangbanger who looked barely out of 3rd grade was chewing on a stick of liquorice. His head shaped like a malformed embryo.
- Joey you found the bathroom yet?
A voice from the toilet ricocheted back off the tiled interior.
- Yeah it's back here. Ritzy!
- Take a damn shit and get a move on.
- What do you want? Lonny asked.
- Money, Freeze, pussy, cock, whatever you got bitch. Whatever you got.
Lonny took a step back.
- She got some fine tits TJ.
Judged one kid. He wasn't wrong either.
- I fucking see 'em.
- We gonna do this bitch or what Teej?
- Kill the dude first.
- Koombaya.
They continued to talk as if Leatherface and Lonny weren't even in the room.
- You sure that's a fuckin' dude Teej?
- Looks like dirty dyke to me.
They all cackled. The kid called TJ poured himself a jugful of lemonade and drank.
- Don't kill the fuck. I got a better idea. Leatherface cringed at the sound of an electric razor buzzing into life. Two mulletheads held him down and TJ started severing off the glued-up fan of Leatherface's Mohawk. He watched as each strand fell to the apartment floor. That lump in his throat reformed itself. TJ flicked off the razor and started pissing himself laughing at the sight of this bald punk. Lonny looked horrified, as if underneath Leatherface's hawk was some hideous scar or something. He felt naked. Vulnerable. Bereaved. On closer inspection TJ appeared to have bad acne. Little craters and flecks of skin ruined his complexion like the surface of some decaying planet. When he zoomed into Leatherface his ugliness on the outside

was startling. Lonny cried out from the back of the apartment.

    - LEAVE HER ALONE! He pleaded.

The kid who'd taken a shit in Lonny's toilet was now watching Lonny's TV with the volume way up. WCN was on.

    - SUICIDE IS AT AN ALL TIME HIGH. CANNIBALISM HAS INCREASED BY 40%. KNIFE ATTACKS AND GUN VIOLENCE ARE UP TO AN ALL TIME HIGH. FREEZE ADDICTION THREATENS TO RUIN SOCIETY ONCE AND FOR ALL. DROP OUTS ARE AT THEIR HIGHEST IN RECENT MEMORY. SO IS THE RATE OF CHILD ABDUCTION, RAPE AND HATE CRIME. SENSE OF COMMUNITY IS AT ITS LOWEST. HERE'S THE WEATHER - JOE…

    - THANKS SUE. AN OPEN HELLMOUTH IS THREATENING TO SUCK WIRE CITY INTO ITS VORTEX AND RELEASE SEVERAL MALEVEALANT COSMIC ENTITIES INTO OUR REALM. RAIN. RAIN. THUNDER AND RAIN. BACK TO SUE.

    - THANKS JOE. DRAKE, WHAT'S THE CURRENT NEWS ON THE COMET HURTLING TOWARDS OUR ATMOSPHERE?

    Leatherface saw a plastic bag come over his head…

****

They dragged Leatherface out into the landing. He noticed for the first time the stink of piss even through the plastic bag. Birds were croodle-crooing all around. TJ led his gang and Leatherface onto the balcony. This building was a death trap. It had open galleries and barely a metre of steel fencing to stop you from falling 16 stories to your death. But had it been made any higher the residents out drying their washing would've looked like inmates behind a prison cage. Leatherface was running low on oxygen but was more worried about Lonny. Where was she? Had those mullethead fucks hurt her?

    - You just a bald fuck now huh?

    - You nothing now? You just a bald-head fuck in leather.

    - A fag!

    - Yeah, a fucking faggot poser!

    - A wannabe punk!

    - Your label has gone bitch.

    - We stripped you of your uniform.

    - Stole back your identity mother fucker!

    - You should just kill yourself faggot!

    Leatherface wanted to talk. He opened his mouth but what he wanted to say was too big to come out and the words stuck in his throat. One kid kicked Leatherface hard up the ass and smashed him over the head with his fist. He never saw which one. Inside the plastic bag was steaming up with hot breath. Everything was getting too hot in there. Sticky too. TJ pulled out a retractable blade and stuck it into the head in a bag. Leatherface yowled as blood began seeping out. There was a grotesque *POP* as the blade caught him straight through the eyeball. TJ pulled the blade back out with a SCHUNK. The pain was sharp but Leatherface was kind of lucky because the socket started quickly puffing up into a bruise, numbing some of the internal pain. The two kids restraining him let go. Leatherface buried his head in his hands and wept tears out of one good eye and wept blood out the other. He finally sobbed. The lump he'd swallowed down twice before had come back bigger and meaner and somehow more un-gulpable. TJ kept laughing as if the thing he was inflicting pain on wasn't even a real person.

- See you around faggot.
- Later poser.
- Nerd!
- College boy.

Then the kids were gone. Leatherface wanted to get back inside to check on Lonny but he couldn't move. He needed a second to himself.

****

Scumbags crawled all over the place. You often found people you knew and trusted were morally reprehensible. Kowalski was well known for its murder rates. People died every other day in that place. Most notably though, Lonny's apartment building had been the crime scene for a mysterious child homicide. A little girl had been poisoned with insecticide, bludgeoned, blinded, raped then spray painted head to toe in gang symbols. Tenants found her plastered back into a hole on the 10nth floor wall. They never found out who did it but the whole city was shaken up about it. Everyone had their own suspicions. Some people put it down to mulletheads - kids killing kids. It explained the gang symbols. Punks got the finger pointed at them too. But there were some people who knew better. People who saw that the gang symbols were nothing but a ruse to throw the cops from the real perpetrator. As it happened Leatherface knew the guy who really did it. An Arab punk who insisted on being nicknamed Raja the Raghead. People were pretty uncomfortable calling him that. It seemed as weird as calling a black guy Leroy the Nigger or a Puerto Rican, Jose the Spic. It just wasn't right. But he was *insistent*. Anyway, Raja confessed everything to Leatherface one night while high on Freeze at an ART/HEROIN/DEATH gig in Lug Nuts. He admitted to having a thing for little girls but that had never been his real driving force and seemed remorseful enough about it all. Raja claimed to be all righteous and holy, explaining to Leatherface that the comet heading to Earth was really the 10nth incarnation of Vishnu sent to rid the world of evil and the desire in him would be gone soon so why not enjoy it before he's cleansed? He only used that as a lame ass excuse for killing kids though. He had a tattoo - यत्कर्म कुरुते तदभिसंपद्यते॥ / *as your deed is, so is your destiny* - inked in Sanskrit across his chest, which seemed to contradict everything he stood for. The gang symbols threw the cops off his scent and Leatherface kept his mouth shut but Raja the Raghead was a sick mother. But he was as good a friend as anyone.

****

An old woman was raking up leaves along the open gallery. Miss Sanchez. She'd seen all this happen to Leatherface and Lonny and didn't do anything about it. She had her own shit to contend with. In Miss Sanchez's opinion, the only thing worse than mulletheads were stinking punks.

Leatherface picked himself up and held the plastic bag to his gaping eye wound. The hallway still reeked of piss but he was getting used to that. He gripped the steel railing and followed it back to Lonny's open apartment door. Furniture was turned over and cans of beans and bottles of beer and soda lay in puddles on the carpet.

- LONNY? He cried out. She didn't reply. Leatherface made his way to the bedroom. Lonny was lying spread-eagled across the bed, blood coming out from between her legs. She was still alive and groaning. Leatherface went over and kneeled beside her. Her cheek was swollen and her lip had gone all fat and purple.

- Lonny, you ok?
- Been better. Fuckin' kids.
- Shit. I'm sorry.

She craned her neck to look at him.

- You're bald Leatherface.
- Yeah.
- Your eye's fucked.
- Listen. We gotta leave the city Lonny.
- And go where?
- Anywhere!
- There isn't anywhere else to go...
- We gotta stop this shit. Stop taking Freeze, stop getting fucked up. Stop behaving like fuckheads. Don't wanna end up like my fuckin dad man.
- Nowhere else to go Leatherface...
- We'll find somewhere.

A new draught travelled along his neck then down the centre of Leatherface's skull where his Mohawk used to be.

- Can't you just talk to me? - Asked the girl.
- About what?
- About Germ. About anything.

Leatherface tried to forget about his missing eye.

- You loved my brother huh?
- I don't know.
- Huh.
- Have you ever been in love?
- I guess.
- Well, tell me what's it like to be in love?
- Hell.
- You heartbroken?
- I guess.
- So what's that like?
- Hard to explain.
- Try?

Her heavy-lidded fish eyes begged.

- I'd have to show you. I'd have to cut your chest open and tickle your guts with a band-saw.
- Dramatic.
- Were gonna have to start whitewashing the windows so when the comet hits were not hideously burnt alive over so many hours. Slowly micro-waved. I'd prefer that.

Leatherface climbed onto the bed and put Lonny's head in his lap still holding the plastic bag to his face.

TRACK 8#

Joss State stood on stage wriggling around in a straightjacket. His band were powering through I MURDER GEEKS while State tried to free himself. The crowd were screaming and spitting at him. He'd been trying to get out of it for 20 minutes and the band were getting tired. Eventually he got out, approached the microphone and resumed the next verse

**I KILL GEEKS WITH A GUN
COS IT'S REALLY VERY FUN
(Riff)
I KILL GEEKS WITH MY BARE HANDS
FOR DISRESPECTING MY AWESOME BAND
(Riff)
I KILL GEEKS WITH A KNIFE
BECAUSE THEY ARE A WASTE OF LIFE
(Riff)
I KILL GEEKS WITH MY COCK
THEY OFTEN FIND THAT QUIT A SHOCK
(Pre-chorus riff)
I KILL GEEKS, THEY BE WEAK,
I KILL GEEKS, EVERY WEEK
I KILL GEEKS, I KILL GEEKS, I KILL GE-E-E-EKS!
(Riff)
IN THEIR MOUTHS**

The fans mimed each verse and baited Joss State to soil the stage - DEFACATE!DEFACATE! - They chanted feverishly like hooligan choir boys in the centre of some Good Friday hymn. MONKEY GLAND were Po-going around in matching green Lycra like humanoid snot monsters. State obeyed his congregations prayer, peeling down his drainpipe's and squatting just over the front-rowers. J.C started doing a drum role as the shit crowned over an expectant crowd member with a ducktail hairstyle and greaser shades on. Pigeon tore out a solo from his custom guitar (*a weathered steam-punk Stratocaster with copper and zinc body, bathed in sulphate for added rust. It looked like it'd been assembled from scrap parts but looked amazing all the same*) Pigeon's hobbies had to interest him and music just edged it, else he would've become a hockey player or something.

After he dropped his load into the fans willingly open mouth, State took some pills that had been tossed onto the stage and shoved them in his mouth without knowing exactly what they were.

****

WIRE-IN HOTEL

He took a big suck of his Jam Cap.

- Shit gig you pigs.

State sounded hoarse like a chain smoker who was in the midst of a minor stroke. He was due on trial in a week for lying to federal agents but wasn't sure if he'd even bother showing up to court. Shooting craps around a coffee table were J.C the drummer and bassist, Krist-500. Pigeon was doing press-ups so hard and fast he almost smashed his face off of the floor with each drop. After State murdered the last guitarist in cold blood, Pigeon was savvy enough to realise he'd better get in shape fast. The Freeze gave him extra energy. They'd stolen Pigeon away from GOD SAVE THE QUEERS and the first thing Joss State said to him upon his initiation was - Don't bring up Rank or you'll be headed the same way.

- I'm gonna go start the taps. I got another shit brewing.

They ended every tour like this - getting wasted and ruining their hotel rooms. Granted they ruined their rooms in a wholly unique fashion - by shitting in every motel toilet without flushing then clogging the sinks with paper and leaving the taps on. To make sure his bowels were full enough to defecate on stage every night and wreck his motel bathroom, State stuck to a strict diet of hamburgers, tacos and sour fruit, occasionally washed down with a tumbler of turbo-lax to keep him in check. His erratic behaviour could have something to do with his upbringing in a remote log cabin in Blue Collar where State's evangelical father often threatened to decapitate his son with a billhook if he ever looked him in the eye.

- Gonna bed.

Slobbered Pigeon.

- What he say?

- Think he's going to bed?

Pigeon nodded.

- Gonna go. Bed.

- Yeah, yeah. Nighty night faggot.

Pigeon staggered to his bed and collapsed. He had these rings under his eyes like someone who'd just gone through an ice-pick lobotomy. Some blood smeared across his Lycra top, not his own. He used to self-harm. He'd mutilated his body with razor blades round about the time he realised he wasn't the centre of the universe. No one else knew or cared but Pigeon was having some seriously suicidal thoughts again. Ready to die of an overdose, ready to succumb to zilch. He just didn't want Joss State to decide for him.

State hollered from the bathroom.

- Those pills I had on stage are making me spin.

A mushroom cloud of Freeze came round the door.

- Shouldn't mix boss. Replied J.C

- Fuck you.

Obscene rasping sounds emerged from the bathroom. They all laughed. Except Pigeon who was still passed out on his bed.

- You a fuckin' shit machine boss! Cackled Krist-500 as he worked Carnauba wax into his palms and started rubbing both hands together. Krist-500 looked kind of like a high school quarterback. He was broad and barrel chested and had a major superiority complex. J.C tossed the dice onto the table and secured some safety pins on his jacket.

- Snake eyes.

- Fuck.

A groan came from the floor. Sylviathe groupie was only just waking up. She'd missed the gig but MONKEY GLAND didn't care as long she was good to go whenever they felt like fucking her. Sylvia was a skinny girl, barely 18 but with the face of a 50 year old drag queen. She had long, scraggy brunette hair and wore a tie-dyed peasant blouse, was mostly found to be braless and always bare-footed. Her wafer thin naked arms were like a skeleton with one coat of flesh coloured paint on it. She was madly in love with Joss State, as many impressionable young things were. Sylvia thought there was a heart inside the brute. Little did she know - there was not.

- Sylvia's up.
- Bout fuckin' time, lazy bitch. State echoed from the bathroom. Sylvia rubbed her eyes with the heel of her hand.
- What time is it?
- Past midnight bitch.
- You played the gig yet?
- Course we played the fucking gig.
- Shit…

J.C was stiff as a hammer. Sylvia roused something deep inside the band, something animal which made them take her on tour as their plaything. J.C stood up from the craps table and moved towards the girl. She was still sitting down beside the bed so J.C knelt down to her level. He tried to keep his voice quiet.

- You wanna make play baby?

Sylvia groaned again.

- The boss gets the first fuck J.C, you know that.
- Yeah well he's taking a mighty huge shit right now.
- So?
- So while were waiting what's say we make play?

Thunder snapped outside the motel window. The weather in Wire sucked. You could be freezing your balls off in the height of summer one day then be stuck to your sheets on a clammy winter night the next. Winter was known to get stickier than a whores bed sheets here. Like a dribbling spastic schizoid it couldn't decide what to do with itself so it just stumbled through the paces pissing everyone off. Mutant weather aside the place sucked anyway. The ghosts on the street were so demoralised by their impending death at the hands of the comet they practically walked through each other. On the sidewalks woman wept with their kids beside homeless junkies and corporate shills. Everyone stood to lose something - a home, a family, a business. Get over yourself huh…

- SHIT MAN. Came State's voice from the bathroom.
- THIS FUCKIN' TOILET PAPER. DUNNO WHETHER TO WIPE MY ASS WITH IT OR DRAW YOU A PICTURE ON IT!

J.C's tongue stuck in his mouth, stuck in its jar.

He stared at the girl. The hollowed slots where Sylvia's eyeballs shot around the room like ping pong balls were ringed with insomnia. Fuelled by paranoia and unrequited love. The girl looked totally wasted. J.C started feeling sorry for Sylvia and decided to back off for now.

****

Leatherface sat in the bath. The water circled in a whirlpool down the drain at the far end of the tub. Lonny walked in and slumped onto the toilet seat next to him. She was just looking blankly at her feet. At her naked toes. Leatherface reached across and put a hand on her foot to comfort her. Morning came with a bone white light outside. Neither had slept yet. How could they? There was a dropper full of Freeze in the bed-sit with an air bubble that rose inside the cylinder like a bobbing eyeball.

- I feel like such a wuss. She said almost laughing.
- Don't be dumb.
- I guess.

Lonny stood up and began undressing. Leatherface squirmed into the furthest reach of the tub to make room for her. She dipped her toe first then slid in the whole foot. Leatherface watched her. In all her nakedness, Lonny's bruises and cuts caught the morning light. Her bellybutton piercing resembled a miniature chandelier dangling above her pubic bone. She curled up into Leatherface's chest and he hugged her. The dirty bathwater lapped at them and a holy daybreak shone in through the casement. They were the only ones left.

- We need to go back to Scarlet House.
- What? Why?
- I want Germ buried properly.
- We can't.
- We can and I'm going.
- I can't go back there Leatherface.
- You won't have to. I'll go.
- That's crazy!
- Jenkins won't be back there. As far as he's aware he killed every punk in Scarlet House.
- And then what huh?
- Then I kill Jenkins and this can end.
- What??
- Relax!
- Don't tell me to relax! You're gonna get killed!
- Gonna get killed anyway Lon.

Lonny said nothing but Leatherface thought she beginning to understand.

- I'm putting an end to this bullshit before I die. Before we all die. I got a purpose now you know?
- What's the point in having a purpose?
- Dunno. What's the point in not having one?
- That's retarded.
- We can all rest in peace once my brother is buried and Jenkins is gone. I'll welcome the fucking comet then.
- You loved Germ?
- Sure. He got me into punk.
- I got *him* into punk.
- Guess I owe you both then. I wasn't a very good brother back you know?
- Hmmm…
- You're agreeing with me?
- I think you loved your brother but you guys were so messed up by your parents you didn't know how to show each other.

- Well now's my chance.

He inspected a cut that ran from his wrist to the crook of his hand. Recent. He didn't know how he got it.

****

- This is your kids last Christmas? Asked Santa.
- Yes.
- Well, now's as good a time as any to tell him it's all bullshit if you ask me.
- Yeah, well I'm not asking you.

Little Carter looked up at his dad with a hurt and confused expression. Dad tried again.

- Come on Santa. Quit messing around.
- I ain't messing around man. Hey Carter, you really think I'm Santa Claus?

Carter nodded.

- Christ. You got your kid brainwashed bub.
- Look asshole, I'm paying you to show my kid a good time. It's his last Christmas and I want it to be a good one. So start making with the presents and X-Mas cheer before I stick my umbrella up your ass.
- Awe jeez... Santa stubbed out his cig.
- Do it.
- Hey Carter, you looking forward to me coming to your house and giving you a load oh great presents...?

The kid nodded, much happier.

- ...Before the comet comes and crushes you on New Year's morning huh? That's 6 whole days of playing with plastic before you're burned to ash...

Carter's dad wrapped his fists tightly around the Santa Clause's suit and exposed a PROMTRAUMA t-shirt underneath.

- Fuckin' meathead!
- Hey buddy, take your kid someplace else ok.

Dad pulled Santa in closer, their noses touching.

- You're dead.
- Newsflash pal - so are you!
- You're dead right now jerk-off!
- Hey Timmy, you maybe wanna help poor Chris Cringle out here and put your old man back on his leash?
- My name's Carter not Timmy...

The kid's dad pulled his arm way back and cracked it forward into Santa's face. An explosion of blood and cartilage sprayed all over a nearby elf. Carter knew his daddy just killed Santa.

****

BLOODY EAR STUDIOS

John Ghoul swirled brandy around in a glass. His leggy, blonde secretary sat in the chair opposite, cross armed. He started talking shit in a half-drunken state.

- Granny was shit scared of the handicapped. - SATAN! She'd scream. - *Ignore Granny* - mom would tell us. But the old bird was right!

- She was?

- Sure she was! It's the end of the world soon isn't it? Satan's coming man, he was always here.

- Disguised as the handicapped?

- You don't get it.

- You're right I don't sir.

Her face was serious. Ghoul decided to leave it. He didn't have to explain himself to a dumb broad (albeit a dumb broad halfway through her PhD thesis!). So he tipped the glass of brandy into his mouth and eyed-up her tits. He had no notion of subtlety nor did he need any. John Ghoul was an old washed up dinosaur - a black, stiff suited relic with a thick, wrinkly neck. He was a ruthless bastard and that's probably why he'd been so successful. It's guys like John Ghoul who helped hurry along Wire's decay.

- Ok baby what you got for me?

- Didn't we just fuck earlier this morning Mr Ghoul?

- No, no you silly girl. I mean *work*. What *work* do you have for me to look at?

- Oh… The secretary picked up her briefcase and brought out a thin folder. She leafed through it till she reached the day's schedule. Ghoul pulled out a hanky that blossomed over his breast pocket and wiped his big hook nose.

- Ah here we are. You got a phone call from Joss State…

- Who?

- Joss State sir. He's a pretty serious client of yours. Makes you a lot of money.

- Ah. Go on.

- He says he still wants the Scarlet House gig to go ahead.

- The what?

- It's a squat house. A dwelling for local punks sir. It's a music venue from time to time…

- Right, right…

- He says his band, that's MONKEY GLAND, needs the gig because they've been removed from another tour date for repeated holliganistic behaviour sir.

- Waa…?

- Hooligans sir, it means they behave like hooligans.

- Of course, yes.

- Well the bands label is also threatening to drop them. That'll be the third in as many years.

- Ok… so?

- So the band need their profile kept up. Gigs are the way for bands to do that Mr Ghoul.

- So why are they telling me about it?

- They want advertising. Fliers, t-shirts, that sort of thing. An extensive viral marketing campaign perhaps?

    - Uh, huh. And when is this "gig"?

    - New Year's Eve Mr Ghoul.

    - You mean…?

    - Yes sir. The night before the comet hits.

    Ghoul sat up in his chair, suddenly interested.

    - This could be huge you know.

    - Yes Mr Ghoul.

    - Profitable.

    - Yes sir.

    - By which I mean very lucrative.

    - I understand Mr Ghoul sir.

    Ghoul got this grin on his face; this corrupt rictus like a Cheshire cat who's just realised the shit in its litter tray is made from gold doubloons.

    - Come give daddy a kiss. Daddy's excited baby.

    The secretary wriggled in her pivot chair uncomfortably as the old dinosaur wormed over to her, lips puckered, hands grappling.

TRACK 9#

It was a heavy night, the kind you get often in the heart of December-Winter. Where the sky seems endlessly black at 4 in the afternoon and crashing aeroplane engines create distant grumbles from above like you're stuck in the metabolic depths of a monster's belly. The night was freezing cold but Leatherface could already feel his throat become scratchy and the onset of nasal clogging long before tonight's exposure. At Scarlet House, choppers circled above, casting spotlights onto the land. Leatherface hid behind a tall tree until they passed the area. The Luftwaffe eventually disappeared. He approached the neglected property of Scarlet House. Lonny had given him a .44 just in case. It was dark but the outdoor sconce fired into bright life casting light onto all the carnage spread out on the lawn. There were blood and body parts everywhere. Leatherface felt nauseous but resisted his urge to puke. He spotted Skittle, bone rods poking out of severed stumps of flesh where his legs used to be. Blood slicked the green like rancid jam, bodies bust apart like slugs dissolved under salt. Fuck, he thought. Leatherface's eyes travelled along the gore strewn grass and saw what he came for – Germ's coffin. It'd been tipped over onto its side, the casket lid ajar with Germ's arm flopping out the corner. Before he had a chance to reach his brother's body, someone fired a gunshot that rang through the night. - PGEEWW! It snapped. Leatherface stood glaring into the forested abyss waiting for the shooter to emerge. The sconce flickered on and off and on and off like a strobe at some druggy rave. He half expected this to happen. Jenkins. He could recognise the lever actioned cough of Buck Jrs slug anywhere. Then he came shuffling out of the shadows

    - WELL, WELL. YOU CAME BACK YE DUMB BASTARD!

    Leatherface took a step back.

    - I just want my brother man. He pleaded. Jenkins gave off this loose, ugly belly laugh.

- SHEEEIT! WELL WHY DIDN'T YOU JUST SAY HUH?

He laughed again, louder, dirtier and more mocking.

- Come on man. I'll leave the city. You'll never see me again!

Leatherface was scared now. His hands were cold and wet and his tickling nausea returned. He thought about reaching for the Magnum tucked into his jacket.

- YOU PUNKS FUCKIN STINK UP MY TOWN. AIN'T NO WAY I'M LETTIN' YA GO FUCK-O!

Jenkins heaved Buck Jr up onto his forearm. His meat red turkey wattle wobbled as he laughed. They looked each other in the eyes. Minutes past. Then - PGEEWW!

Leatherface got a round fired through him.

He fell to his knees then folded over onto his back. Jenkins boots crunched under the soil and crispy grass. Looming over Leatherface the cop grinned and left.

****

He was going to die and he knew it. Leatherface found he really rather liked the thought of dying. Of being dead. If someone asked him if the thought of dying was an appealing one before all this, he would've replied with a grin and given a little head slant before insisting that his sincere opinion was that life was precious and therefore worth living. But now he'd been shot. Lying paralysed on the sea fringe, Leatherface felt like he'd just risen from a plague pit. All the dirt and bodies of his comrades were stretched out in one mass grave. They looked peaceful enough, crumpled in comfortable positions, wading motionless by the water. One body, Cutter maybe, wasn't quit over the finish line yet. Poor bastard. He twitched like a dreaming dog, his face in a mask of blood. The thought of dying or being dead was pretty attractive now. His hair had grown in a little - even and naturally blonde. Not how he imagined. A corpse seemed serene, incapable of violent acts or violent thought. A cancelled vessel ready to decompose to soil. He missed Lex.

A cockroach scuttled towards Leatherface staring at him with an eyeless glare. He fucking hated insects. Leatherface felt fear overcome all numbness as the sensation of the roaches pincers scuttling over a bare hand drew from him his first reflex in some time. He wanted to claw at himself but his body was still partially paralysed. He spotted a shard of broken glass and began mentally preparing himself for the possibility that he might need to cut into himself should the roach decided to enter his body. Then he doesn't feel the roach. It's gone. Leatherface remembers being shot - his gun-holding hand sagging. The lead .44 weighing him down. His wound wetted through his t-shirt, body crumpling into two halves. The impact of the lead bullet feeling as brief and superficial as a gelatine paint gun capsule. The shooter thumbing his nose and running off like a damned lowlife coward. This was a fucking massacre. But he felt better about the unwinding clock of consciousness than he did about the long, dull, terrifying waiting room of life. He doesn't remember being a kid but knew he must've been one once. The hassle. It was Christmas Day. Fuck - he must've thought.

****

A yuppie guy hailed a taxi and it pulled up onto the curb. He was conservatively dressed, had brush cut hair and carried a Samsonite case. He seemed well-to-do enough if a little uptight.

- Take me to the theatre district cabby.

- You got it.

The yuppie pulled out a bottle of aspirin, shook out two pills and popped them into his mouth. He watched the 24/7 storefronts whiz past the speeding taxi and felt hungry.

At midtown Wire the yuppie climbed out the cab and tossed the driver a 20 and told him to keep the change.

- Gee, thanks mister.

- Forget about it. Happy holidays.

- Same to you pal.

The all-night delicatessen attracted him like a fly to a lantern with its neon glow. A guy wandered the streets dressed like a huge cruller, selling pastries and hotdogs from a vending tray. Suddenly the yuppie wasn't so hungry. Inside he browsed the top shelf magazines and opened the cooler at the frozen counter pretending to buy milk. It was all a plan. He checked the shop keep who was flicking through a dirty magazine. Ghetto-tech music thrummed from a portable radio. The yuppie clicked open his case revealing a disassembled shotgun packed into protective foam. He started building up the gun with intent of blowing the shop-keep away.

- Hey buddy. What you doing over there? Hollered a voice from the bagging area. The yuppie panicked. He screwed on the nozzle and buried the gun into his trench coat and started walking towards the till.

- You gonna buy something buddy huh?

The yuppie hefted the gun out, cocked it, snapped the smoothbore and fired one slug right into the shop owner's face sending him flying backwards into a slushy machine.

- H-H-H-HAPPY HOLIDAYS!

He looked at the hole where the old owner's face used to be and started smiling. The face was like a bloody blancmange, a deformed tulip in blossom. Besides an old condemned building, outside was the dark midtown porno theatre. There was no one at the box office marquee so the yuppie jumped the turnstile and headed down the dimly lit hallway to screen room 3. He felt nothing. He'd never killed anyone before but would've felt the same had he decided to let the shop keep live.

****

Ad-ware popped up on the computer screen.

- **BUY AND WIN! CLICK TO WIN!**

- **COMET FALL-OUT SHELTERS, $50**

Lonny switched off the screen. She turned on the TV and saw that an old transmission of SCARLOT HARLOTS playing on Channel zero. They were doing SICK? from W.A.R.T

-

I'M SO SICK OF TEENAGERS
ONE MORE LOVE SONG AND I'M THROUGH
I'M SICK TO DEATH OF ROMANCE
AND I'M OH SO SICK OF YOU

SICK!SICK!SICK!

SCHADENFREUDE

I'M BORED TO TEARS OF POLITICS
I'VE SEEN ENOUGH OF WAR
A RACIST FROM THE HITLER YOUTH
ARYAN, NAZI COR-PO-RATE WHORE

SICK!SICK!SICK! SICK?

Lonny wasn't in the mood for aggression right now. Figures. She still felt a little shaken up after those street kids had barged their way in and raped her. Things were creaking outside on the landing. She needed extra locks for the apartment door. Noises outside, like men with the horn, stags ready for mating season, butting with their antlers, screaming for a red deer. Needed more weapons too. For protection. She'd given her only .44 to Leatherface. Why did she let him go alone? Probably cos Lonny couldn't stand the thought of returning to Scarlet House. Couldn't stomach seeing Germ's lifeless corpse with his frozen-open bug eyes judging her even in death. Seeing that face she'd let down so many times.

- *You should've gone with him Lon.* He'd say.

Lonny knew she could be selfish. Of course she knew that. Her constant fucking around with other punks pretty much proved it. But the more she thought about it the more she realised she only fucked around because she was scared. Scared of settling. Scared of actually loving someone and being content with that. See, Lonny was anarcho-punk and didn't believe in shit like love or normalcy. Since her dad kicked her out for failing the Easton University entrance exam, Lonny had only ever been motivated by chaos and a desire to see modern suburban life crash and burn all around her. That sounds pretentious but it wasn't like that for her. Daddy's neglect had soured her right through. She became hard as a popcorn kernel, hollow as husk from a fruit. When it was announced that a 7 mile wide asteroid was on its way to Earth it seemed her prayers had been answered.

Fuck you dad!

Fuck you Easton University!

For a while Lonny revelled, making merry of the ensuing global apocalypse with genuine sincerity. But that attitude didn't last. She met Germ, someone who didn't seem altogether glad that everyone was going to die. Germ was more about music and people getting along. He may've been suicidal but Germ didn't want to take everyone with him. His reasons were personal and he dealt with them in a personal way by killing himself.

The news flashed up on the TV. OFFICER JENKINS MAKES LIEUTENANT AFTER SQUAT-HOUSE RAID!

- MAKING LIEUTENANT ON THE LAST MONTH OF HUMAN EXISTENCE IS VERY EXCITING FOR ME. AH'M A'HAPPY!

Lonny could feel herself changing. She was bored of being such a cold, hard-ass. She missed Leatherface. Was he ok? Great timing to get sentimental. Growing a heart in the wake of the worlds end. Figures.

****

MONKEY GLAND entered BLOODY EAR Studios and hopped the lift to floor 6. Joss State was anxious. He'd been fucked by agents and labels before so went into the proposed meeting more than a little sceptical. They needed this gig.

- This cunt better get us the fuckin gig.

- He will. J.C reassured his boss.

- Else I'll cut out his throat.

The lift pinged open at floor 6 and they got out. Sylvia wandered towards a vending machine and the band went on without her. They came to a door that read - MR JOHN GHOUL/TALENT AGENT.

- Must be the place.

State tore the door open without knocking and revealed Ghoul and his secretary fucking across his desk.

- Uh…gentlemen…I…

His secretary pulled herself away, yanked up her panties and brushed down her suit.

- Your 12 o'clock mister Ghoul. She said.

- Oh right. Of course, I…

- We're early.

- Yes, yes. That's fine I…um…just let me get myself together…

Krist-500 advanced on the quivering agent.

- Scarlet House. New Year's Eve. You swing us some merch? Some publicity?

- I certainly think we can arrange…

- No. State burst in.

- No?

- Listen fuck-head. This has to happen and we need every motherfucker from Wire to Spittle to know about it.

- I see.

- Yeah, so I figure you'll try and fuck us.

- Fuck you?

- Yeah. I know your type fuck head.

- You do huh?

- Damn straight. I tell you my conditions.

- Alright I'm listening.

- We don't pay you a thing. You pay *us* to play and you get the word around we're playing.

- That's not a very tempting offer.

- Wasn't meant to be an offer. It's a fuckin demand. I killed Salvador Props cosa this shit.

Krist-500 pulled out a 9mm and stuck the muzzle into Ghouls neck.

- Capeesh?

- Uh huh. Sure, Ok.

Pigeon started laughing hysterically for no good reason.

- Will you shut him up!

State was becoming impatient. He wanted the preparations done and dusted. What was up with Pigeon anyway? Krist-500 clobbered Pigeon over the back of the skull with the gun butt and he fell to the floor like a loose bag of potatoes.

- Why the rush to get this gig? I don't know if you're aware but…

- Oh I'm aware pal. I'm aware plenty ok. I got a surprise for the crowd.

- What?
- Something bigger than the comet.
- That so? Ghoul sat up in his pivot chair.
- I'm gonna kill myself onstage. Columbian necktie. J.C is gonna cut my throat and rip my tongue out through the hole in my neck.

J.C, regaining consciousness added,
- Escobar style…
- Isn't that a bit…gimmicky? Ghoul leaned back again.
- Yeah so?

The secretary guffawed out loud.
- What you lookin at ya dumb blonde bitch huh?
- I've actually just done my thesis on vagina dentate in popular Western culture. Dumb wouldn't be an accurate insult.
- Vagina wah? Sounds lame.
- I suspected you might think that.

The 6th floor of BLOODY EAR studios was the second highest point in the whole of Wire. It was estimated that whenever the comet picked up speed towards the city that this would be the first property destroyed.

Then…

A blinding light shot through the glass panels and shook them till they shattered. Everyone dropped to the ground. The building began to rumble and quake.
- WHAT THE FUCK'S GOING ON?
- THE COMET'S HERE ALREADY!

A hunk of debris crashed onto John Ghoul, flattening him so all that stuck out were his slick shoes. MONKEY GLAND crawled for the exit but were halted in their tracks by a screeching voice.
- I'M NOT A CHEERLEADER!

A sound like a hot air balloon detonating popped and rasped and Ghouls desk caught fire. Standing up, behind the flames, the secretary tore open her suit jacket. She stood bare chested with a twisted face as plaster crumbled away all around her like something from a fucked up horror movie. The secretary - the antichrist! The secretary started pointing and singing MUTANT CUNT lyrics.
- FUCK ALMIGHTY, THE COMET'S COMING BUT WE DON'T CARE!

TRACK 10#
OUTRO

NOT NEW YEAR'S EVE -

Wire city was flooded with people. Almost exactly midnight. People pouring into the streets. People on ledges and balconies all stared at the sky. Naked display dummies gazed up from storefront windows. People clogged into the subways abandoned kiosk. A shoe-shiner

with his bottles of polish and cans of stain stopped asking people if they wanted service. You'd have thought they were all watching some natural phenomenon as celebrated and mysterious as an eclipse. Not a speeding locomotive ready to burn a crater into the Earth's crust. A girl bent over a pool table with her skirt hiked up to her waist and got slapped awake by a brutal, hairy hand. The flaming ball grew in the distance from a dot to a beach ball to a blinding sun. In the electrics shop doorway a scammer folded up his stand of camcorders, sunglasses and damp porno magazines and foolishly tried to run. There was nowhere to run. The cars gridlocked on the freeway, got nowhere either because the roads from Wire never led anywhere else except Spittle. The comet picked up pace. All the clefts of its surface becoming more visible. An old wise-cracker took a drag through his stoma. The heat intensified. Quicker…
Closer…

Then suddenly the raging bull decelerated. Slowed to the point of stillness. The burning ball hovered, all serene, metres from the capitol building's weather vane.

Lonny watched on. Kids in people carriers on the way back from hockey practice got out and gawked. It wasn't even New Year yet! Grease monkeys' legs were still sticking out from underneath their car's furnaces. Oblivious. The sphere stretched away off into the distance and made it look like the sky was falling, like a blanket was coming down to cover up the city. There was the sound of mechanics, shifting gears and bolts grinding together. Then a small doorway appeared at the centre of the comet. People started to speculate - ALIENS?

A voice soon emerged from the sky to correct them, one that boomed and almost deafened the people who heard it. The voice said…

- **THAT LOW HUH?**

BONUS TRACK

I'm here at a hamburger joint called NICE BUNZ by the railroad outside the demolished interstate. The name is misleading because the buns in NICE BUNZ are stale. I normally come in for coffee and a muffin but on this occasion I've splashed out on some wings and a bag of sliders. The neighbourhood is sketchy even for Spittle. Oral sex contests aren't unheard of here. The waitress has no teeth and it's not a friendly atmosphere. Across the table from me, some kook is stubbing a Freeze butt onto his wrist and smiling to himself. My DOUBLE DOUBLE arrives with a pubic hair coiling out the cream. My wings taste like shit, like they've been quickly nuked in a microwave. NICE BUNZ is a rat-hole even for a city spiritually and economically crushed by recent revelation. This isn't a good place to be and I sure don't come for the eats. I come because it's where my favourite band met each other. Let me get to the gut issue…

Spittle has produced some fine bands. Some important bands. Here, in NICE BUNZ, chewing on tepid wings and avoiding eye contact with my waitress at the bar, I want to discuss one band in particular who make me forget about all the shit around me.

RADICAL FAERIES debut EP, LANDSHARK ATTACK is a criminally underrated example of pre-comet Spittle's queer punk scene. A bunch of straight-edge, gay humanoids with a dark sense of humour. The murder ballad PUSSIES LOVE PUSSY is an example of this humour (we think!), where the band fantasise about a world where heterosexuals are condemned then brutally killed in concentration camps. In a way, their fantasies were to prove grim prophecy. The Spittle slackers have only a 4 song demo to show for all their efforts before they disbanded and this is a shame.

Life could've been very different for these boys.

In spite of spearheading a revolution, no one knows who they are. Savage and sensitive they never did get the success LANDSHARK ATTACK richly deserved. Instead, they have been banished to the racks and shelves of unsigned art-punk obscurity. In light of former guitarist Leatherface's recent passing, this reporter feels it only fair that RADICAL FAERIES receives some publicity, if only to atone for our own previous ignorance.

The Band…

Front man Johnny Sexism was a strange character. Gargling his lyrics from behind hair curtains, sounding like a young boy who's just swallowed a volley of teargas. The guitar screech of Leatherface was as sharp and startling as a jagged pencil to the solar plexus. An assault in 4/4.

Wry and unpretentious even with a name like RADICAL FAERIES, they specialised in a very unique kind of noise. It wasn't good. Not by most people's standards was it considered "good". But it was the principle that made them relevant. The result - a combination of laconic thrash songs and dissonant jangle-pop. Band motto - If you don't like us who the fuck cares? These are words to live by.

> *I NEVER ASKED TO BE QUEER*
> *TO LIVE MY LIFE IN CONSTANT FEAR*
> *BUT MY MOMMA SAID I GOT AN OVERSIZED MOUTH*
> *PERFECT FOR SUCKING AND BLOWING DOWN SOUTH*
> *AND AN ASSHOLE THAT COULD STAGE SWORDFIGHTS*
> *AND I ALWAYS LOOKED A LOT BETTER IN TIGHTS*
> *AND AN EYE FOR A DRUG AND THE MIND OF A THUG*
> *AND A DICK THAT COULDN'T SATISFY A VIRGIN LADYBUG*

What of the existing members? Well, there are none. Johnny Sexism died of AIDS, which he contracted when a hetero fan spat into his mouth. He tried to commit suicide by blowing his brains out but somehow survived it. Needless to say, what with his newly deformed face and the AIDS at such an advanced stage, Johnny died a pretty unhappy boy. The bassist, Zombie, formed a blues folk band and subsequently chopped off his own ears, killing him 4 hours later in a Spittle hospital bed after a long, painful bleed out. No one was by his side. Mange the drummer was probably the worst drummer to pick up sticks. He was off-time and always distracted by a guy in the crowd he wanted to fuck. But man, that guy gave everything. He raped that fucking drum kit every night and got so loud with it he was constantly replacing the skins. Then poor Leatherface. Last I heard, he was a cabbie in Spittle before the pigs got to him. Typical! Leatherface finds his recognition now he's dead and gone and unable to enjoy it. That's life though.

That day. NOT New Year's Eve as was promised. Everything became of secondary importance. It's just like RADICAL FAERIES predicted. Down to the last terrible detail - Clouds of Syphilis will appear and tear lesions in the sky's eye and blood will pour from above and deep in all its plasma, within each red cell is all of our hate, all of our folly, yours, mine, holding it all together until it crashes down on top of us. Like rain. Like tears. Then the world falls foul to an endemic of cardiac arrests. People start dropping in the streets, clutching their chests, gasping for air. I'm convulsing on the hot tarmac, my face landed right next to a pyramid of dog shit.

Figures…

MAN-GOGOL-DOG

Originaly published in Sein Und Werden

A Labrador sat next to me on a park bench wearing a Hawaiian shirt and lipstick the colour of shocking pink – a bitch, I think. She opens up a book called "HOW TO SELF LOBOTOMISE" with a picture of my face, wide with surprise, on the dust-jacket. She sees me reading over her shoulder and shields the book against her chest all offended. I suddenly feel the collar tighten around my neck - the short, sharp tug of my owner bringing me to heel.

- Chris, come on now, bad dog!

I squat over a balding patch of grass and go number two. My owner pats me on the head and scoops up my faeces with both hands.

- Good boy!

A bird flies down from the branch of a sycamore, spotted wings winking like a butterfly's. He looks at me disdainfully, the way most inner city fowl do.

I hear hoofs clopping behind me - a giant suburban coyote atop a saddled horse.

The parks activity is always crazy like this on a Sunday afternoon.

The traffic lights ping to green and a hoard of cockroaches scuttle across the road. My owner and I follow suite. We continue along 5th Avenue on our way back to the apartment. In the window I see the striking similarity between master and pet. We're both fragile boned and narrow faced with a wispy streak of dowdy hair wilting over a windshield forehead. We're both pasty skinned (we're both completely naked). We even have the same tattoos – a portrait of dear old mother spread over our left butt cheeks.

I guess the old saying is true - we really do start to look alike after a while.

Outside a storefront we bump into a woman I vaguely recognise, from where I can't remember. I listen to the incomprehensible dialogue exchanged between the two.

- Ah Chris, how are you?

To which my owner replies…

- Not too bad, yourself?

She then says something which appears to anger my owner. After a sharp intake of breath, we walk away with the familiar woman calling after us.

My owner tightens my leash around a clenched fist.

The air is cold against my pink, hairless flesh. I'm eager to get home for a bowl of kibble.

Only a couple more blocks to go

On the television screen I see my face on every channel. We approach the precipice of a large manhole with a luminous sign saying "EXIT HERE!" I'm compelled to inspect what's down there, but my master violently yanks me away. Aggravated by his constant restrictions I turn on the master, gnawing on his forearm as he attempts to guard himself from attack. A white rage blinds me. A spray of blood spurts into my face when I penetrate his skin. I drag master's lifeless body across the city, shaking him around like a beat up chew toy. I make it back to the park where it's my intention to consume my owner once and for all. To finally be free of the leash...

Giraffes and Spaniels are watching me maul my owner in a rabid display.

When I realise he's dead, torn to shreds, I look up at the sky. The clouds part and I see a face I recognise.

- Good boy - says a voice.

SOMNAMBULIST - SOUTHSIDE

Originally published in Polluto magazine, 2012

Jerry looked in the mirror. He used to be a movie star.

His face was long and drawn like a starving reptile and Jerry's absent stare suggested all the traumas of a man who'd just fallen soul first into a river of leeches…

He had a beard of shaving foam which leaked from his chin. Living in the Southside of Hell was actually working out ok for Jerry. He moved there when L.A lost its edge and just never looked back. Sure, you get a lot of demons and monsters and people you really hated when you were alive roaming around on the sidewalks outside, but it still beat the killer responsibility of having a pulse.

Unlike most people who wind up here, Jerry came to Hell of his own volition. It's easier than you might think. You just gotta find an apartment, get a job and you're good to go. It really was that simple for him.

Jerry began popping his knuckles. He placed a finger and thumb on his neck then on the limp of his wrist just to check he really was still dead – *nothing* – thank god!

The phone rang from the living room; he let it go straight to voicemail. A hysterical woman spoke, shrill, indignant, thoroughly pissed off. Could've been his mother, his sister, his girl or any strange woman Jerry come into contact with – that's a broad canvas of strange women in Jerry's case.

He did well in Hell. Demon girls could se
in his eyes the awful places he'd been and they found this an alluring quality of his.

Jerry dragged the razor blade through the cloud of foam until the colours changed from bright white to dark red. Outside a train hurtled past, shaking the whole apartment. He'd missed his ride to work. It meant he'd have to jump a thorny tailed dragon across the lake of fire. Jerry made ends meet by clipping recently deceased Wall Street yuppies' cigars for them in a high rise downtown – but like I said, he used to be an actor so he kissed ass convincingly.

Jerry matted a layer of shaving cream into his chest hair and lathered it into foam. He took his razor, poised it and dragged the blade against the grain until blood bubbled through. The cut from his cheek continued to bleed, dripped onto the bathroom tiles. The slash across his chest wept like Mary, a reservoir of blood forming neatly at his feet. Jerry unbuckled his pants and let them fall to his ankles. He squirted a dollop of shaving cream into his hands and mixed it into the wiry shrub of his pubic hair. He picked up the razor – took a breath – and dragged it across the base of his penis.

Jerry had completely changed his image, he had to. He was so sick of everyone watching him ALL THE TIME. After filming the Box office bomb "Too Cruel for School", he packed up his things and came Southside. Jerry's hair had been bleached by the burning sphere, which hung over Hell's terrain but it used to be black when he walked amongst the living. Jerry tried every mask he could until he finally found one which fit just right – ditching the peck implants sure helped. He was able to form a gut, a turkeys wattle, sores and acne scarring and a true sense of himself.

He'd also gone by a different name but no-one could remember what it used to be. This was fine as long as they stopped watching him...

MY DAD THE CARPENTER

The wooden boy who lives in my attic always used to watch me jack off.

Each night he'd peer through the vent which looks down onto my room and begin chuckling to himself maniacally. This didn't stop me whacking away mind you. I was nineteen - even a possessed, prying Pinocchio couldn't put me off masturbating when I got the urge.

He didn't frighten me at first. To be honest I didn't see him as much of a threat. I was doing the poor creature a favour. How else could it get its perverse kick? I had no curiosities regarding his origin and no desire to inspect the attic space he roamed around in. I didn't bother telling anyone about this either because frankly, who the hell would believe a word of it?

It was a unique and voyeuristic relationship - we both understood each other's roles. While I beat off to a porno, he'd get to sit and watch through the slats and laugh away as I disgorged a measure of warm jism over myself.

He stayed up there and I stayed down here.

Things were fine.

But when my dad made me go up to the attic to bring down a load of empty cardboard boxes for mom's yard sale, I betrayed the role I'd been playing for so long. The attic was his territory – not mine.

I'd ruined our game…

Now…

Its eyes a vicious red, its nostrils flared and snot filled, its teeth like crooked gravestones sunk in gum - I've never known a face like it. Up close, the wooden boy seemed a million times more malevolent and terrifying.

Several pictures of Rory the cat are up here, not that there aren't just as many downstairs. The cat is worshipped in this household – unlike I am. He just sits around licking his balls all day but gets treated like a prince. The cat deserves this more than I do.

I'm staring through the window in the attic. The moon is a hot white, curled into a perfect crescent. My gut twists into a tight knot. Its breath is like nothing I've ever smelled before – like sour meat, it's almost sulphuric, turpentine-esque, rotted fruit in a room full of new furniture – total death breath.

For the past few minutes, it's just been staring at me. My gaze remains firmly on the moons arch outside. I'm frozen to the corner of the attic.

The wooden boy starts hyperventilating, drooling and gasping up large breath-fulls of air.

If I don't look at it then it isn't there.

But he is there…

He's always been there…

I can hear its long talons scrape on the attic floor, dragging the deformed upper-body towards me with each heave. It's right in my face now, its breath melting away my tears of fright.

- You really like to jack off huh? – He says, slobbering all over his chin. I nod. The

117

wooden boy inches even closer. He inhales the air around me like a dog picking the scent of a bitch.

- You stink of it.
- I'm nineteen. I do it a lot…
- I'm not complaining, just saying.

Now I'm thinking the wooden boy wants to rape me right here in the attic, squash me into a corner and start bearing down on me while he makes me, well, you know…

- You scared?

I nod.

- You're real cute when you're scared.

The moon catches one of his large marble eye balls reflecting the dead, heartless essence inside its hollow cadaver. Amidst the attic sea of sealed boxes, photos of Rory and old toys I spot something. It's a picture frame. My dad is in it smiling and holding up two pieces of plywood. The boy sees me looking at the picture.

- Father sent you to me.
- What?
- He made me so I could watch over you.

My mouth goes cotton dry. The muscles in my throat want to swallow but there's no available saliva. Sweat lines the crooks of my palms. It's hard to breathe. My head hurts. My heart beats frantically in the microwave of my chest.

- Why?
- You can't keep your hands off of yourself. It's not natural. Your mind is in the gutter! You've fallen behind in school. Your mind is never away from your own pleasure. You've been given three years to clean up your act, get your head screwed on…
- I can change! I can stop jacking off!

It laughs loudly as if the very notion is absurd.

The wooden boy has a tongue that isn't made of wood like the rest of him. It's like a cats tongue, short and bristly and bumpy. He draws it along my cheek. My toes curl in tight and my calf muscles flex. My spine experiences a cold wash of static that tenses my sphincter into a tiny O.

- Are…are you gonna…
- Gonna what? – The wooden boy starts exhaling again, all excited.
- You know?
- What, fuck you?

I nod again. The boy starts laughing again covering me all over with his foul stink.

- I may have sentience but I lack certain…anatomical requirements!

He points to his groin.

- My dad wouldn't do this…

Even I don't believe this claim!

- He's not your dad. He's my dad now. That was the deal
- What deal?

The fog of confusion thickens around me and sheer panic sends my mind into the realms of desperate insanity. Fear still has a firm stranglehold on me but I'm angry because I'm so confused. I lift myself up, sweep my right arm back and propel it forward into the wooden boy's hideous mug.

It makes a noise like the crack of a rifle shot – my wanking arm.

(For posterity, I would like to leave some pearls of wisdom behind regarding a subject that I believe I am qualified to represent.

THE DANGER WANK: *a highly risky form of masturbation with heightened climactic effect. Unbuckle your trousers and get a good speed going. Then shout your mother to come upstairs - doing this will require an increase in polishing speed. The aim is to finish before your mother's unceremonious entrance. Very pleasurable if successful.*)

His face splinters and breaks as he flies across the attic and crashes into the opposite wall beneath the window.

I'm sure my hand breaks on impact too. I don't know why but I feel more concerned about my masturbatory patterns being disrupted - I can't jack off with a broken hand.

The boy doesn't get back up. I go over and scoop up his corpse, pull the chord of the attic door and descend the ladders.

I'm so angry.

I feel so utterly betrayed. My own father for Christ sakes!

I storm into the living room and see my parents snuggled up on the sofa watching Letterman. In a blind fury, I toss the wooden boy's body into the centre of the living room, right in front of the television set.

- Explain that!

My dad gets up. I can see every pore on his skin as he sticks his face into mine. I can see the gin blossoms on his cheeks and nose. I stay defiant.

- I want to know why you did this…

My dad just grins and sits back down next to my mother.

- Is it because I didn't want to be a carpenter like you? Huh dad, is that it?

- No.

- Is it because touching yourself is bad is that it, huh?

- No.

- Then what? Why would you do something this evil and fucked up?

My dad pointed to Rory the cat who was sitting on a satin pillow by the fire. Rory was nursing his ass and looking pretty pissed off and violated. Then I knew why my dad did what he did.

- You fuck with the cat you fuck with me boy, and watch your language…

THE WORM GOD

Originally published in Dead Man's Tome

Cherry Island

If you fly over the border of sea which divides Chile from Tahiti, just left of Easter Island, you will see a strange landmass in the shape of a grimacing skull.

Don't be fooled by its soft, welcoming name, Cherry island is a dark and terrifying place where its indigenous population frequently indulge in acts of rape, cannibalism and any other insidious habit they care to luxuriate in. Best described as a mecca of sinister commerce in the mould of Gomorrah, Cherry Island is nicknamed "The Cay of Scum"…

Come on in already…

A stink will wriggle up each nostril like some evil smelling cheese - even through the iron peanut shell of a Boeing, you'll smell it. From 10,000 f.t Cherry Islands Nubian-esque pyramids stand like tall arrowheads, the thick verdant greens of strange and exotic orchids provide a fringe of colour above the pebble strewn gravel sand.

On the island *nothing* is sacrosanct.

A huge ship docks in the bay – a royal vessel with the island's insignia on the hull (a sea monster devouring a female). The shipmen jump from their apertures, plopping in the ocean foam of the coastline and begin advancing towards dry land. Their cargo is 50 crates of golden wine stolen from Santiago city, and of course 25 Chilean children snatched from their beds. When the large berthing door creaks open, each crew member starts ushering the frightened children out into the water. The pirates are all ugly, disfigured men who would surely not be allowed to enjoy the free world had they been situated anywhere else.

John Langsyne watches this from the safety of a distant cove. He's a journalist; some might argue he's as crooked as the pirates, if less equipped to handle himself. On his way to cover Jacques Chirac's latest visit to Tahiti, the plane suddenly plummeted from the sky somewhere over the Polynesian triangle. When Langsyne's parachute disengaged, the wind carried him over to Cherry Island. While on his slow descent, Langsyne saw the far off mushroom cloud of the plain as it struck the ocean – there could be no other survivors.

So here he is, alone with only his journalistic integrity to keep him warm at night, in which case he can expect die of pneumonia soon enough.

Langsyne's mind isn't on an exclusive scoop, his fear is too great - this from a man who once infiltrated the Lebanese border alongside a band of Syrian troops.

Conceived at Chhatrapur, Orissa, in British India, Langsyne's father was a member of the Indian Civil Service. His mother was chief engineer of the Madras Railways. Both parents were deeply disappointed in their son.

The pirates appear to have offloaded their cargo, wine and children are now gathered on the gravelly bank of sand. Langsyne sees one of the children being hit with the butt of a gun because he won't stop crying. The others promptly cease their disputation. The children are led behind a dark reef of vines leading to the Anoka jungles heart.

Suddenly, John Langsyne's instincts return. He *has* to follow the pirates. It should be noted that Langsyne is not driven by his sense of human empathy or an intrinsic desire to see justice prevail. He follows purely from the point of self-sufficiency.

****

A peal of thunder overhead forces Langsyne to shelter under a Bakke leaf he finds wilting in the tropical savannah heat. He drinks water from his flask and continued on through the haze of trees. The coming of night brings a nightmarish edge to proceedings. Deeper into the abyss, Langsyne relies on instinct alone to see him through the midnight hours for the nocturnal animals of Anoka were silent and lethal. There is no air of progress here, only stagnant things that refuse to grow or evolve.

He sparks a hissing flare and uses its red glow to light the way through the thick jungle. A colossal statue made with blood stained stone. On it are elaborate hieroglyphs detailing tribesman's battle against the illustrious worm god. John, being sceptical of all folklore, is dismissive of its existence. But the longer he spends in the jungle, the more pungent the stench of children's blood becomes. It's this knowledge which gives credence to his current apprehensions.

****

Langsyne forges westwards, journeying through the Amazonian heart of Anoka jungle – completely alone. Motivated by his desire to get a great story he pushes on. Anoka jungle attacks his senses with bright colour and strange sounds; though the dense undergrowth has begun thinning a little at least.

He'd heard that often town warriors would declare war on the worm. This was, of course, a foolish decision – the kind of decision typical among the strong of arm and weak of mind. The worm's attacks were random and seemingly motiveless. John, becoming increasingly caught up in the myth, wanted to locate then destroy the larvae it birthed into the subterraneous depths of Anoka. Only then could the city be free of its parasitic reign. Langsyne becomes aware of a sense of compassion swell within him – he is equally as terrified by it as he is by the threat of the Worm God.

John tries to rest for a while beneath the gibbous moons lunar light, extracting leeches from every corner of his body. He pulls a cluster of red berries from a branch and shoves them in his mouth. He can't remember which types of berry are safe to eat, but hunger has ruled over reason. The next morning, John spears some Cherry Island fish heading upstream and eats them on the bone.

It has been three days and Langsyne begins to doubt the larvae's existence entirely. Weighed down by his sack of supplies, Langsyne is hours away from dropping dead in the middle of nowhere, dehydrated and utterly hopeless – until he comes to a clearing. The absence of forest has given distinct path to a darkened temple ahead. Rejuvenated by this discovery, John Langsyne ambles forth.

Beneath his feet, he feels a change in terrain. The insect infested lowland soil and course weeds begin to smooth out. He senses this is significant somehow. Langsyne almost feels the presence of the unholy mutated grub festering nearby. He's so excited by this new success that he barely gives a second thought to his empty water flask.

The air grows increasingly humid the closer to the temple John got – more so than in the tropical centre of Anoka. Vines climb to the apex. He cuts through a tapestry of vegetation all the while trying to maintain his optimism. John is dry and thirsty, he cannot deny this knowledge. He feels his eye lids scratch together when he blinks and his lips start to crack. On top of all this, John feels his stomach grate which he begins to assume are the effects of the berries he'd consumed a few nights earlier. Instinctively, he reaches for the flask which he forgets is void of sustenance. The onset of complete exhaustion forces Langsyne to rest a moment.

- Bastard's son. He curses.

The water in Anoka is supposedly undrinkable, polluted by the worm's amniotic fluid. So John Langsyne is already preparing himself for the possibility he may need to drink his own urine. He hears trees falling in the distance.

Peering back into the labyrinthine webs of the jungle, he feels a ****

Sweat sears down John's face as he tries to process what he's just seen. Anoka is alive with noise again. His body aches for water and the evident lack of any nearby is driving him insane. John decides to continue on past the dark temple and into last stretch of Anoka.

By now, he knows he is as good as dead. Although he has made it this far into the jungle, he cannot make it back out the way he came. John pushes deeper into the core until the clearing ends and the ominous forest returns. Guided by celestial light, Langsyne is certain he knows which direction to take. But when he turns to face the temple, it has gone. He searches frantically around him, but it has completely vanished. John's dismay becomes enflamed further when he realises the clearing was now full of giant exotic trees and vines – much like that of Anoka. He's back in the overgrown jungle, with all its denseness and horror. The vegetation seems greater now, somehow more congested. There is an evident progress here which was absent before. The music of the night is different too. Before, John could've identified a small majority of the Anoka wildlife's grunts and growls, but now they're more varied, more obscure. Hideous beasts lurk beneath every shadow, no longer hiding places of mere insect or amphibian. John is fenced in with these beasts by the immense vines and weeds which swell around him. He shakes off a cramp that travels down the course of his left arm.

- Fuckin' berries!

A sudden numbness fills John's mouth. He tries to produce saliva but is unable. He tries to scream but the tongue is dead in its cave. Panicked by his loss of feeling, Langsyne begins sticking Bakke leaves into his mouth in the hope that the mild poison from their fleshy roots will help to return some glimmer of sensation. But the more Bakke he fills himself with, the more he seems to be incapable of tasting it. John is struck with as much regret as he is fear. He should never have eaten those berries. Now, they will be the death of him. John wanted to come to Anoka to prove a point or die like a hero trying. Instead, he'd collapse – dead, forgotten, neck bloated from poison, with his tongue lolling out onto the undergrowth. There was no honour in that.

As John falls to his knees, the sound of trickling water sparks life into him. He gets to his feet, drool now dangling from his numbed lips. He parts a tall thicket of reeds and sees the murky jungle pond in all its glory. The water is black with suspended sediment. John feels dizzy but ecstatic all at once. His only urge is to bathe and drink from the water and he is a slave to these urges. He strips off and dips his toe into the layer of green scum which sheets the ponds surface. The rest of John Langsyne followed.

Thigh deep in the water, he wades forward until it became less shallow, at which point he immerses his head. The worm's amniotic fluid seems harmless enough. John could even admit to feeling its benefits as he laps up handfuls into his mouth. While he can't taste the water, he nevertheless feels replenished by it.

Eyes watch him with interest.

Kholo notices ripples in the water where the spinal column of a croc weaved in and out. Every part of Anoka despised the smell of human beings and sought to eliminate it from its pores in any way necessary.

Carefully, he gets back out trying not to disturb the water surface. The crocodile is oblivious and doesn't swim anywhere near him. When John turns back the croc has resurfaced onto the mud bank on the opposite side of the lake. It sits on its hindquarters staring back at Kholo. He looks at its face, at its long mandible packed with razor sharp triangles, its smooth belly, and sees in its dead eyes – the presence of the worm god. Langsyne suspects he will be struck down at any time, so moves further west.

****

The worm god is conspiring against John, he knows it - the way he'd seen it manipulate Anoka to swallow intruders. Perhaps the worm's worshippers have the right idea. They appear immune to its wrath. As John considers this, the suns orb grows fiery red and he feels its heat burn and peel the skin from his bare back. Rays shine down onto the Anoka, melting leaves to pulp and slowing down jungle predators in their tracks. John feels every animal in the jungle watching him undercover. Just as it seems the night will never leave Anoka, the sun fires into brilliant, searing life with a vengeance. At least John has been nourished, which might keep him on his feet at least a little while longer.

The jungle goes on forever, the vines and plants blossomed into huge, intimidating organisms and John's hope begins to die once more. He's so hungry. He has to hunt down, catch and kill something. John was so unpopular in Detroit, he couldn't get service I restaurants. He'd read enough to have a vague idea what was required of him.

Langsyne uses his limited tribal initiative to fashion some rudimentary spears, shaving shreds of wood from tree bark and tying a sharpened stone to the tip with sinew. He uses Bakke sap to poison the edge and he is ready.

****

Fumbling its way through the forest is an eight legged insect with a body fat from insatiable greed – an insect you'd only find on Cherry Island. Behind a shrub of leaves, John stalks his prey. The hideous insect moves in such a way that suggests its skinny legs struggle to carry the sheer weight of its body. It doesn't travel more than ten yards at a time without stopping to rest and gobble up more of the jungles defenceless basin dwelling critters. John sees his moment and tosses the spear. To his obvious disappointment, it strikes the large insect on the leg and breaks apart. The insect moves through the leaves, blissfully unaware that something was hunting it. He has failed and night is preparing to fall heavy.

****

John Langsyne sits on the dirt and looks at the blistering sun and the awful lunar body of the moon lying dormant behind it. In a fit of madness, triggered by exhaustion and malnourishment, he begins chewing at his own hand. The poisoned berries have made his flesh supple and his bones brittle so he has no trouble biting off and grinding up large quantities of himself. John feels no pain for his nerves are dead with poison and his mouth numb with the same reaction. The mental shock is muted by the onset of hallucination. Although John has begun self-cannibalising his own body, to his drug saturated eyes, he believes he is making love to three of the nude females from the darkened temple. He kisses them hard on their mouths and cups the global mounds of their breasts and slides his fingers between their thighs and smells the fresh absence of human sex on their flesh and hair. John feels his groin tingle with life and the sense of old habits returning. The worm grows fatter in its breechcloth. On the mud bank the croc watches with cruel relish. Children are cowering somewhere nearby under the raised blade of a pirates knife. The worm god got him…

TRAGIC TRUTHS OF JOHNNY O'DRISCALL

(Kafka with toilet humour)

Johnny O'Driscall scored the winning penalty for Scotland in the world cup final against England at the San Siro. Johnny then jetted back home to play Hampden Park, supporting a recently reformed Black Flag in front of 60,000 adoring fans...

...but that was just a dream

Johnny O'Driscall once got 6 numbers on the lottery, including the bonus ball, bought a Porsche and married the high school prom queen...

...but that was just a dream

Johnny O'Driscall woke up one morning to discover himself travelling through a truck-drivers colon. After waves of muscular contraction, O'Driscall was eventually expelled - via the anal canal - through the rectum and then plopped out into a toilet bowl full of murky water. All his life Johnny thought he was a real person with real dreams, but it turns out he was just a piece of partially digested shit who dreamt he was a man...

...this is his revelation...

Johnny opened his eyes and saw the ceramic around him. He looked up and saw the sinister winking eye of the truck driver's asshole. Johnny kept looking upward as the truck driver reeled off a sheet of paper and stuck it between both hairy cheeks. Johnny watched as the crumpled ball of paper parachuted into the bowl, landing right beside him. Suddenly the water began to bubble and foam up like a Jacuzzi before a vacuum started sucking him under.

Just before he'd been pinched off, Johnny felt everything warm and familiar around him flood with cold light. Before he knew what's what, he was half sunk in the gas station toilet. The last thing he remembers seeing is the asinine grin of the driver and the expression of pride on his face as he stared back at Johnny.

Now, being pulled through the pipes, Johnny felt the harsh fear of realising everything he'd once known about himself was completely false. The truth of the matter - Johnny had no sense of who he was or even where he was. He figured he'd probably only been fully formed hours ago. He was a turd, a turd that'd unfortunately been granted sentience.

As Johnny floated along the city bay he stared forlornly into the firmament. A rusty soda can bobbed beside him, smiling cheerfully

- Hey man. Where you headed?

- Wherever the current takes me I guess.

- Gee, you sure look sad bout something? Penny for your thoughts?

Johnny sighed theatrically. The soda can introduced himself as Bob.

- I wanted to be a poet or a great philosopher.

- Who's to say you can't be that?

- My situation pretty much dictates that all I'll ever amount to is a piece of shit.

- But you can rise above that, set an example. Great minds are all made from something right? Yours is just comprised of chicken wings and Twinkie's instead of flesh and bone.

Johnny squinted.

- That's a kind of reductionist theory isn't it?

- Hey man, if you wanna float through the rest of your life a worthless, lazy turd then by all means…

Johnny considered this while watching a swarm of seagulls tear south. Bob's ring pull had fallen off and the rust of his aluminium body was getting worse.

- What can I do? It's not like I got legs!

- I believe in fate man. Wherever you end up, it's where fate wanted you to be.

Bob seemed to make a lot of sense.

- I mean, take a look at me. I been drained of all my content, crushed, kicked and thrown in the trash. I been duked open and tossed aside. But I don't let it get me down.

- No?

- Hell no! I'm gonna be an elevator repair-can.

- How you gonna do that?

- Don't know yet. But you can kiss my shiny ass if you think I'm gonna happily bump along to Frisco with you, doing diddly squat with my life.

Johnny saw the sun break the peak of a distant garbage pile. He felt invigorated by a renewed sense of himself.

- You know Bob, you're a real optimist.

- You bet your ass I am.

- But I'm happy bumping along. I think it was just the shock of…you know?

- Discovering you're a piece of shit?

- Yeah, but now I've given it time to settle in, I think I'm gonna be ok with it.

A gust of wind lifted Bob into the opposite stream, taking him away from Johnny.

- Hey, looks like this where I get off.

Johnny watched Bob disappear and returned to his quiet reflections.

- I'm a piece of shit, said Johnny.

BIG D AND THE KID

In the kid's bag they found nothing but innocent things. The usual kinds of thing you might find in a 12 year olds rucksack - old candy wrappers, a prepared lunch in a brown grocery bag, one crumpled up football jersey and some worse for wear comic books. Harmless shit. Big D tossed the pack into the backseat. Eddie the driver tried to keep his eyes fastened to the road. In the back, the kid was squirming around like crazy. Tom was making a half-hearted effort to restrain the boy in his seat but something in his face suggested he was plain out of his depth on this one. Kidnapping kids was a whole new level of sleaze. The wee guy was like one of those idyllic children you see dolled up for pageants - jet black bowl cut and cow eyes above all suspicion. Big D reached into his pocket and retrieved a handgun. Fear through suggestion maybe? Not a chance with Big D. There was tension in the car as it jerked over broken rocks scattered on the dirt track. He started polishing its muzzle. Almost at once the kid began freaking out and Tom begged the boss to put the damn thing away.

- He's seen too much Tommy - Big D sympathised, feeding bullets into the barrel cylinder and cocking the neck

- Kids seen too much - Eddie and Tom shared a glance in the rear-view. This was getting too heavy. Kidnapping little kids was never on either of their minds. How had it come to this? But Big-D, well that guy was losing it. Why did this have to happen? Why did they snatch the kid in the first place? Big D rolled over and dismantled the headrest so he could look into the little kids' eyes. Tom's heart jumped as the gun rose into view and his boss took aim. Eddie screeched the car to a halt.

- What ye doin? -

Eddie's head hung loose over the steering wheel, staring at his feet resting on the gas pedal.

- EDDIE? DRIVE! - But God bless Eddie he wouldn't start up the engine. Big D eventually rolled back over, his face twisted with hurt in the face of the crony's disobedience.

- When were done wi the kid, you're gonna get a little surprise Eddie pal - Big D gestured with his gun. The driver looked worried. Threats from Big D usually met his word. In an instant the boss had reaffirmed his aim and sent a whipping lead cylinder into the kid's forehead. A wet shell of red paint spattered up the back window, over

The seat and all over Tom. Big D maintained his dead calmness. Tom shrunk into the corner of the car. Eddie cowered away, shielding himself from his boss who was now prodding the gun against the driver's cheek.

- What did I tell ye Ed. You don't mess wi Big D -

Blubbering, Eddie begged the boss not to pull the trigger. A heavy-duty lorry hurtled past sounding it's klaxon to Big D's bemusement. Rather than blast his brains out through his ears, Big D took rare mercy on Ed and blew two bullets into each of his knee-caps. A faint mewling from the driver betrayed the true extremity of pain doled out. Tom quaked in the back beside the little kid's detonated corpse. He wiped away the boy's blood with the cuff of his sleeve. Tom could taste it on his tongue and immediately started spitting all over himself to try to banish the flavour. He felt drenched by it. Eddie leapt onto Big D's back and tried wrestling the weapon out of his hand. Ed began rapping quick, rabbit punches into the boss's skull until the posterior area of bone gave way to bloody yoghurt…

MEDUSA HEAD

The medusa head in my hands
Like a green football
Serpent hair wriggling between my fingers
Every gorgon I've ever known
Even ones who said they loved me
Are hated of mortal man
Her ritual mask
Of stinking seaweed
Gasps for air
Maddened by lust
Then
Through a gravely syllable of laughter
She says
I'm not afraid of you
I defy you
I have a penis
The wings on my sandals stop flapping
I turn the medusa head
And see her castrating scowl
Caravaggio's shrieking masterpiece
A face for women's rage
Her eyes catch me
My biggest mistake
I see the Real
The sad reality of the universe
Of me
I've lived my life happy in fiction
In the boneyard of thought
Now I'm turned to stone

LET'S SPEND SOME TIME TOGETHER

CHARACTERS -

GEORGE - Husband of Llewellyn, father of David and Merlyn. Upwardly mobile, highly educated middle-aged specimen

LLEWELLYN - Wife of George, mother of David and Merlyn. Equally as successful as her husband though appears to have aged better.

DAVID - Son of George and Llewellyn

MERLYN - Son of George and Llewellyn

WILLIAM - Next door neighbour. Attractive school teacher with whom Llewellyn has had secret relations.

BETTY - Williams wife. Utterly enamoured by her husband. Openly sexual and often discusses she and Williams past exploits.

MIA - George and Llewellyn's shiatsu

TERRY - William and Betty's boxer

(David and Merlyn are in their parent's bedroom trying on clothes and mimicking their behaviour)

David - This could fatally compromise my reputation.

Merlyn - If I cared about reputations I wouldn't have asked you to come to my apartment.

David - True. I'm sorry for being so unforgivably late...

Merlyn - So shouldn't you start getting undressed?

David - I was waiting for you.

Merlyn - Well then you shouldn't be so presumptuous.

David - On the contrary, I...

Merlyn - I suppose you think because I'm a woman I can't keep my pants on?

David - What? No of course not!

Merlyn - Really?

David - Really. I have the utmost respect for you Llewellyn. Surely my offer of tickets to see L'italiana in Algeri at the Pavilion should've settled your apprehensions about me?

Merlyn - But George...you are a wealthy and notorious solicitor of prostitutes...

(Both boys burst into hysterics. Merlyn adjusts his mother's straw sun hat that was half a head size too large for him. David has on a work shirt and tie and revelled in his carnivalesque performance imitating their father.)

Merlyn - They don't really wear this shit do they?

David - I'm not sure milady, but you can be certain of one thing?

Merlyn - And what's that George?

David - that they couldn't pray to pull off such attire as fitfully as you or I?

(David runs a finger along the lengthwise crease of his father's Fedora and arches his arm into a

teapot handle for Merlyn to link arms with.)

David - What would you say? Burroughs? Bogart? Gene Kelly?
Merlyn - Oh George you are awful!

(Llewellyn and George are sitting in the living room. David is looking for something while his wife dusts furniture)

George - Have you seen my book Llewellyn?
Llewellyn - Well which one?
George - The Bukowski one?
Llewellyn - Tales Of Ordinary Madness?
George - No the other one…
Llewellyn - No I've not seen it George.
George - But it was right here on the sill…
Llewellyn - Well I haven't touched it if that's what you're suggesting.
George - I'm suggesting nothing Llewellyn, simply that it was here on the sill and now it is absent from the sill.
Llewellyn - Well did you take it to the toilet with you?
George - No I don't think so.
Llewellyn - Well double check then…
George - No. I definitely didn't take it in there with me. I'm 100% on that.
Llewellyn - How can you be sure if you don't check? I once misplaced a bottle of Merlyn's formula. I sat it on the kitchen table and I was so sure I'd left it there that I didn't see the point in looking elsewhere. Do you know where I found it?
George - No but I'm sure it was earth shattering…
Llewellyn - I found it behind the sink. Can you believe that?
George - Are you still having trouble sleeping Llewellyn?
Llewellyn - A little why?
George - Maybe you should tell yourself that story.

(Llewellyn sprays some perfume on herself then squeezes out a cloud of it into the air before thrusting her face into it.)

Llewellyn - Maybe I'll just borrow one of your books. If you could remember where on earth you left them. Why don't you just check the toilet George?
George - But I'm 100% on this.
Llewellyn - You would be George.
George - I'm reading a Burgess novel in the toilet you see.
Llewellyn - Which one? Earthly Powers?
George - No. The other one.
Llewellyn - Clockwork Orange?
George - No, no of course not.
Llewellyn - Well it's not in the place you left it so all I can suggest is look elsewhere George.
George - Yes. Perhaps it's in the boiler room or down the plughole.

Llewellyn - Don't be facetious.

(George sits ruminating motionlessly. Llewellyn tuts and glares at her husband.)

Llewellyn - If you find this piece of literature so indispensable then perhaps you ought to take better care of your things. You never see me losing books.

(George continues to gape into space. He's fixed, trapped by dead thoughts of nothing in particular sucking him in as if his tie were caught in the conveyor belt of some lethal machinery.)

Llewellyn - You shouldn't stare into space. It's impolite.

(George rises to his feet.)

George - Should I never release my gaze from you then my sweetest sapphire?

(Llewellyn frowns.)

Llewellyn - Fuck sake…

(George straightens his spine in anger.)

George - You're making me feel impotent again!
Llewellyn - Impotent?
George - Yes, impotent.

(Llewellyn chuckles indignantly.)

Llewellyn - Lord…
George - Keep that castrating scowl too.
Llewellyn - Are you feeling well?
George - No. That's no thanks to you.
Llewellyn - Even your smiles seem queasy these days…
George - When was the last time you saw one of those from me?

(Merlyn and David enter. Merlyn is nursing his brother's hand facing the palm towards the ceiling. Llewellyn sits back down, her gaze still focused on her husband. George appears equally transfixed by a spot on the coffee table. David leads Merlyn into the kitchen where the sound of drawers sliding open and much rummaging about irritates Llewellyn.)

Llewellyn - What's going on in there?
David - Where are the plasters mother?
Llewellyn - Have you tried in the toilet?

(George snaps back to attention not wanting to miss an opportunity.)

George - Maybe the lost sway pearls of King John's royal treasures are in the toilet as well **Llewellyn**? Or a Caribbean barge buried deep within the depths of its mysterious murky waters?
Llewellyn - You make me sigh, you really do make me sigh.

(George begins sniffing the air, snorting.)

George - Your perfume smells ghastly woman!

Llewellyn - If it keeps you away from me then it's achieved its function.

(She fiddles with her thumbs. George smiles.)

George - Hungry for it aren't you?

Llewellyn - Shut up George.

George - Maybe one day they'll make a film about your life Llewellyn. A story of urban and domestic brutality about an underclass drug addict who meets a tragic end, discovered with a dropper full of clotted blood sticking out of her blue arm.

Llewellyn - And starring, oh I don't know - Marty Feldman's exhumed corpse as her bulgy eyed, deadbeat husband who drove her to it all.

(Merlin and David re-enter the living room, the latter boys hand completely bandaged up but still seeping blood. They depart from the intense living room atmosphere where their parents are slowly and publicly killing each other. George pours port into a glass and raises it.)

George - Still going through with your Vag-icide?

Llewellyn - I really wish you'd stop calling it that. I'm having my tubes tied. That's it.

George - And who have you got doing it?

Llewellyn - Dr Lakeland.

George - That unscrupulous scalpel jockey?

Llewellyn - She's cheaper and a friend. Unless you'd rather perform the operation yourself?

George - I'd rather stick my head in the oven than go down there.

(He gestures towards his wife's lap. This seems to hit Llewellyn deeper than the other insults. She has become used to these bitter exchanges but was always under the impression that they still found one another physically desirable after all these years. Even in the remotest possible way. It was why they were still together she thought. Wasn't it?)

(George and William are watching football on the telly. Llewellyn, still sore about her husband's low blow, decides to ruin his night.)

Llewellyn - George did you find your book?

George - What? No.

(George says this without turning to his wife. William opens a can of lager and sups the foam. William is a good looking man, tall with dark hair. A teacher at Merlyn and David's school. Llewellyn and William had previously had a sexual encounter at one of George's cocktail mixers. Safe to say it meant nothing to either Llewellyn or William. But after George's deep rejection the night before, Llewellyn is left longing to expose her dirty secret. To rub her affair in George's face. To show him other men find her desirable. Still find her desirable. To make him green with envy. William is indeed attractive and a competent love maker to. He looks a bit like a young Mathew Broderick - full lipped, ashen faced and boyish even at the wrong end of 30.)

Llewellyn - Did you tell William about your fiasco?

George - What? No Llewellyn.

Llewellyn - Why not?

(George ignores her and reaches for a can.)

Llewellyn - He might find it unreservedly amusing.

(George's mouth twitches. She is getting to him now.)

Llewellyn - George won't you tell William about your fiasco? You know the one about the vanishing Bukowski?

(George stands up and tosses his lager to the floor sending a spray of foam over William.)

George – CAN'T YOU ALLOW ME A MOMENTS PEACE TO ENJOY THIS? WILL YOU DENY ME EVEN THIS?

(George's voice echoes. She has succeeded in getting a rise. The house is silent. So silent you can hear shelves groaning under the weight of thick, hardback books. William, seeing an opening adds himself to George's side of the argument.)

William - At least she doesn't cart you around like a fuckin convict on remand every day, traipsing through discount stores and lingerie sections!
George - OH BUT SHE DOES WILLIAM! SHE DOES!
William - Really? I had no idea I apologise. Women eh?
George - AND THAT'S NOT ALL SHE DOES TO ME! OOOOH NOOO! WHEN THERE'S FOOTBALL ON THE TELLY SHE WANTS TO DO SOMETHING! LET'S SPEND TIME TOGETHER GEORGE! LET'S BE A FAMILY GEORGE!
William - Enough to make you sick…

(Again there is silence.)

William - How're the boys?
Llewellyn - Who? Oh…they're fine…

(At William and Betty's the following night, George and Llewellyn eat their meals quietly. Egg and chips ala Dunbartonshire housewife. William and Betty are a notoriously sexual couple. After 4 years of marriage their love making can still be heard through the drywall and the family home is awash with European and African erotic imagery. George stares at a picture of a native holding his long dark penis in two hands like a rope tied around his waist between mouthfuls of egg.)

(Llewellyn and George's shiatsu, Mia, and William and Betty's boxer, Terry, play out back. Both families suddenly notice a yelp coming from behind the patio door. Llewellyn and George's dog has mounted William and Betty's dog. An awkward silence fills the room as Terry allows Mia the bitch to hump his left leg. After opening the door and summoning their respective pets back inside, Mia begins dragging her rear along the carpet. George giggles.)

George - They do say dogs start to behave like their owners…

(Llewellyn tries to apologise.)

Llewellyn - I'm ever so sorry…

(Will and Betty both give a big dirty laugh. Mary veers off into another topic.)

Betty - Will and I went to the Bahamas once.

(William nods.)

William - We made love in the ocean.

(Betty starts giggling in fond recollection.)

William - We split off from the tour group.
Betty - It was the 700th time I'd seen William's penis in that month alone.
William - 700th time you sucked it too.

(As George stuffs his face Llewellyn tries to respond and keep from unravelling.)

Llewellyn - How wonderful for you both.
Betty - Well sex is the work of my soul, and it's the work and passion of William too.
William - And when you satisfy the individual's soul you satisfy the universes soul.

(Mia and Terry both lay licking themselves in the sun. Terry turns to his shiatsu lover, running his tongue across her mane and says.)

Terry - She described him once as an "a po-faced cunt"…
Mia - A what? - Asked Mia, jerking her head away from the pink, lapping tongue wetting her hair into a fringe.
Terry - A "cunt" Mia.
Mia - And what is…a "cunt"?
Terry - An effective expletive and course noun meaning female genitalia. Quit effective.
Mia - Hmm…cunt eh?
Terry - Perhaps we should incorporate more course nouns into our vocabulary.

(Back in the dining room George and Llewellyn have snapped.)

Llewellyn - At least I degrade you in private.

(Llewellyn has now started pouring copious amounts of rosé wine into a champagne flute.)

George - No, no. You degrade me subtly in public.
Llewellyn - I find you nerve shredding irritating and I've been unfaithful but that's your doing surely you can see that?

(William, with a guilty look on his face tries to vindicate himself of blame.)

William - You maimed her. I just fucked her.

YOU SHOULD'VE JUST GOTTEN HIM THAT NINJA TURTLE

Christmas Eve…

Fred teased the barrel of the gun with his fingertip.

A minute before he'd cocked the barrel into Santa's face.

A minute before that he'd fed a long silver bullet into its chamber.

- Fred, please… begged Santa amidst a jolly chorus of nervous laughter.

- Can-it cringle!

Fred released the safety to prove he wasn't kidding around.

Santa gulped. His hat sat at an angle revealing an area of balding scalp beneath. There was blood all over his string vest and he had a busted lip that bled through a clot. He had two dark bruises covering each eye, his lids weighed down heavy making it difficult to see clearly. He stared down the nozzle of Fred's gun.

Santa began to plead with his captor.

- Please, Fred, don't do this

Fred guffawed. His eyes shot around the garden shed maniacally and the gun remained pushed into Santa's grill.

- You don't have to do this!

- You didn't have to ignore my list!

- I didn't ignore your list!

- Then why didn't I get my Donatello ninja turtle, huh? Answer me!

Santa bowed his chin into his chest.

- I didn't ignore it Fred, I just…

Fred knelt to Santa's level, staring him deep in the eye.

- You just what?

- I…

- Go ahead say it! You just didn't think I deserved it that year, right?

Santa hesitantly nodded to confirm.

Fred pulled himself back up.

He went over to his father's power tools which rested on a high shelf.

- You self-righteous monster. You gave me hope. You can't play god like that, you know? It's not right. It's not fair. I blamed my parents. Now they're dead and their bloods on your hands cringle you sick fuck…

Fred climbed the shelf and retrieved a heavy toolbox.

- What're you doing Fred? - asked Santa, now trying desperately to squirm out of the rope knotting him to his chair.

Fred didn't reply.

He brought down a hacksaw. Santa squealed with fright.
- You know, I loved Donatello the most man…
Fred began advancing on the lassoed saint. He pulled the light chord dangling from the ceiling and the bulb burnt out to darkness.